"IF YOU NEED HELP FINDING THE BED, I CAN OBLIGE . . ."

Blair caught Abby's hand in an iron grip before she could do any damage. He pulled her so close that she was aware of every inch of his muscular strength through the thin fabric of her evening blouse and skirt.

"Don't try that again," he warned, the last word barely uttered before his mouth came down on hers in a punishing kiss. Abby tried to draw back, gasping in protest, but the brief parting of her lips was all Blair needed to harden his assault. His devastating probing undermined her control completely, and suddenly resistance was the last thing on her mind. . . .

SIGNET Romances by Glenna Finley

WANTED
FOR LOVE

by
Glenna Finley

We'll hunt down love together
—SWINBURNE

Ⓞ
A SIGNET BOOK
NEW AMERICAN LIBRARY
TIMES MIRROR

For Elizabeth

PUBLISHER'S NOTE

This novel is a work of fiction. Names, characters, places, and incidents are either the product of the author's imagination or are used fictitiously, and any resemblance to actual persons, living or dead, events, or locales is entirely coincidental.

SIGNET TRADEMARK REG. U.S. PAT. OFF. AND FOREIGN COUNTRIES
REGISTERED TRADEMARK—MARCA REGISTRADA
HECHO EN CHICAGO, U.S.A.

SIGNET, SIGNET CLASSIC, MENTOR, PLUME, MERIDIAN AND NAL BOOKS
are published by The New American Library, Inc.,
1633 Broadway, New York, New York 10019

First Printing, September, 1983

1   2   3   4   5   6   7   8   9

PRINTED IN THE UNITED STATES OF AMERICA

Chapter One

"You can't be serious!"

Abigail Trent stared with exasperation at the gray-haired man beside her who continued to stroke a small owl, blandly ignoring the fact that he'd just thrown a mammoth-sized monkey wrench into her vacation plans. "I don't want to spend my time in Bermuda looking up Blair Morley," she went on. "In fact, if I'd known he was still there, I'd have chosen Nassau for my trip instead."

Her uncle snorted to show what he thought of that and put the barn owl back in a nearby cage which was furnished with a turkish towel, a water dish, and another barn owl who watched the goings-on without ruffling a feather. The pair of beautifully marked brown-and-white birds was so striking that Abigail forgot her annoyance for a moment and said, "You did a marvelous job raising these two."

"Mmmm." Jonas Trent's gruffness couldn't hide his pleasure at her compliment. "Only trouble is, when they come in so young, there's the devil to pay trying to get them back in the real world. Barney especially." He nodded toward the bird he'd been stroking. "By now, he thinks that a mouse served for breakfast is his due. Lord knows how he'll feel about working for his groceries."

"You'll figure it out." Abigail glanced around the room lined with wire cages which was the main section of her uncle's wild-bird clinic. "And to think you're supposed to be retired! You've never worked harder in your life."

"I've had some good people to help me. Blair was one of my best assistants."

"I knew we'd get back to him." Abigail reached over and picked up a syringe, filling it from a jar of strained veal, green beans, and margarine. Automatically she squirted the mixture into the open beak of a baby robin who was sitting hopefully in a nearby cage and then put the syringe back on a tray for the next feeding. "Too bad that Blair concentrated on feathered females," she said dryly. "Somebody should have told him there were other kinds of birds on the block."

"Be fair, Abby. He didn't need any lessons handling women. There seemed to be plenty of them dropping in when he worked here. I've never had so many offers of volunteer help as I did then."

"Some women will do anything to be seen with a man," Abigail sniffed, wishing that somehow they could get off the topic of Blair Morley once and for all. It was bad enough to have to figure out a way to avoid him in Bermuda—let alone rake up ancient history that she preferred to forget. "Are you serious about my getting in touch with him again?"

"I certainly am. There's a report that I need to get to him and it's silly to risk losing it in the mail when you're going to be right on the spot. Besides, I've already talked to Blair and told him that you're coming." Jonas reached in a small refrigerator at the end of the room and pulled out a platter with pieces of beef heart on it. "It's time to feed outside and I'll have to hurry if I beat the rain. Why don't you go and put some coffee on?"

"Sure you don't need me to help?"

A wintry smile passed over her uncle's lean features. "That great horned owl caged by the garage isn't one to tangle with. I'd hate to have you leave on vacation bearing scars a bikini wouldn't cover."

She nodded. "He's all yours. I could hear him snapping his beak when I walked by the cage earlier."

Jonas pursed his lips thoughtfully. "He *is* a little irascible. Doesn't take much to set him off, so I won't hang around. There's some cinnamon bread if you feel like making toast with the coffee."

"I'll have it ready."

Abigail watched him go, carrying his platter of beef hearts for the owl as well as an open can of kitty salmon for the caged seagull who was recuperating from a wing injury. She checked to make sure the baby robin was all right and that the door on the barn owls' cage was securely fastened before she headed for the kitchen of

7

her uncle's modern brick rambler, overlooking the deep blue waters of Puget Sound and the scenic San Juan islands. The house was on the edge of a village which had sprung up around a ferry landing but still was surrounded by enough trees and green lawn to make Abigail feel that she was in the country. It had been a home away from home for her during her university years. She'd happily spent her holidays and between-term vacations with her bachelor uncle, as her father's job with an aircraft company meant that her parents were usually overseas. Jonas Trent had coped surprisingly well in the substitute-parent role. In fact, everything had gone smoothly until her college-graduation year, when Blair Morley had appeared as Jonas' assistant.

Abigail heated the water and got out coffee mugs automatically, her thoughts treacherously going back to that earlier time. Strange that it was still so vivid after almost a year and a half—but then, Blair Morley wasn't the kind of man that a woman would forget, even though she'd been a continent away in the intervening months.

Not that Blair had ever done anything to attract her attention. Not once, she recalled, with a strange sense of desolation. The day they'd met, he'd acknowledged Jonas' introduction with a courteous nod and gone on writing—as if her arrival were of considerably less importance than the wounded pair of crows he was observing in the clinic just then.

His studied lack of interest both annoyed and intrigued her because, in her own way, Abigail was a rare bird, too. At twenty-two, she possessed a trim figure, coppery gold hair, and eyes of even deeper blue than the waters of the Sound, which were just beyond the bulkhead. The result was a delectable specimen of modern womanhood. She'd had it confirmed during her four years at college, where she'd had more than her share of proposals—of all kinds. She had turned them all down; the matrimonial ones politely, the other kind firmly because the men involved didn't interest her.

It was a little different when Blair had taken one look all those months ago and obviously relegated her to the bottom of his priority list. And it must have been quite a list because Blair was the kind of man who'd rate a second look from any woman. It was hard to ignore a lean six-foot male who moved with such ease and assurance— even in jeans and a blue chambray workshirt with rolled-up sleeves. He was dark-haired with high cheekbones, and a tight jawline that looked as formidable as Gibraltar. In case anybody missed its rocklike quality, his gray-eyed gaze possessed a piercing quality much like the hawks in Jonas' cages. There was one difference, though; Blair hadn't needed talons to rip her ego to shreds. He'd just stood by like a superior bird of prey and let her accomplish that all by herself!

The teakettle on the stove let out a shrill whistle at that moment and Abigail moved over to take it off the heat, pouring the boiling water over instant coffee in the two mugs. She put the kettle to one side and stood staring at the steaming liquid, remembering almost bitterly how coffee had been part of that last night, too.

It had been her birthday and Jonas had planned a combination birthday and graduation dinner to celebrate.

He'd arranged it at his private club in town—allowing Abigail to invite her college friends in addition to family acquaintances he'd selected. It had been a wonderful idea—except that at the last minute, Jonas hadn't been able to come. He'd sent Blair to deputize for him—but it was a Blair dressed in a dark suit and crisp white shirt, suddenly looking older than the six- or seven-year edge he had on Abigail. As the evening progressed, most of the younger women had to be pried away from his side. It wasn't surprising; Blair rated head and shoulders over their dates without trying.

As the hostess, Abby did her best to make sure that the neglected males weren't completely bereft of attention, attempting to convince herself that her motives were altruistic. She stuck with that story just long enough to thoroughly annoy Blair, who discovered her putting on her coat by the front door toward the end of the evening.

"Where in the hell do you think you're going?" he asked, sounding exasperated.

"Out." She waved a hand airily. "With Jerry. To get some air."

Blair caught her as she tried to move by him. "Jerry can go by himself. You'd do better to concentrate on black coffee in the kitchen unless you're low on manners as well as high on champagne."

"Are you intimating that I've had my limit?" Abigail started out on a dignified note but a hiccup punctuating the sentence brought an even grimmer line to Blair's mouth.

He didn't break the heavy silence that followed until another hiccup surfaced in the quiet hallway.

"Damn!" she muttered resentfully.

"Exactly," he said, choosing to misinterpret her reaction. "You'd have been better off to concentrate on eating rather than drinking dinner."

"I didn't plan . . ." Her voice trailed off when she realized she'd been about to confess that she'd lost her appetite early in the evening—about the time he'd passed her by to dance with a brunette who'd clung tighter than plastic wrap. After that, Abby was determined to show him what a wonderful time she was having with her partners. Unfortunately, she lost count of how many times the obliging waiters had topped off her champagne glass.

Blair must have spent all his spare time keeping track.

She lifted her chin defiantly. "Didn't you have anything better to do?"

"No, dammit! I promised Jonas I'd keep an eye on you. That's why I'm here."

"I didn't think it was because you liked the party," she said, letting her annoyance show. Another hiccup made her plunge on recklessly. "Well, you can go off duty anytime so far as I'm concerned. I'll be fine as soon as I get some fresh air. Jerry's waiting outside—"

Blair cut calmly into her words. "Not any longer. I told him I'd handle the task."

"Then you've one hell of a nerve!" she flared. "I can certainly take care of myself."

"Including driving home?"

"Of course." The words were out before she remembered that she'd been counting on her uncle for a ride home since her own car was in the garage over the weekend. A quick look at Blair showed that he hadn't moved and his resigned expression indicated that Jonas had added chauffeur to his duty roster. Abigail took a deep breath and tried to sound in control of the situation. "Jerry can drop me off later. All I have to do is ask him."

Blair shook his head and sounded as if he were trying to hang on to his patience. "Jerry got the idea the first time. I told Jonas I'd see you home, so that's what's going to happen. Now, I'd suggest you go in and wash your face with some cold water."

"Why?" She stared at him uncomprehendingly. "Is there something wrong with my makeup?"

"No, but cold water might help you to see things more clearly. You'll want to say good night to the rest of your guests before we leave."

His tone of disdain was twice as effective as ice water and managed to squelch Abigail's hiccups in the bargain. "I'd planned on it," she managed finally. "If that doesn't interfere with your plans for the rest of the night."

"Just so it doesn't take longer than another fifteen minutes." He put a firm hand at her back and guided her toward the dining room and the music. The three-piece combo was still in the midst of a Latin-American number when they arrived and, without asking, Blair slid his arm around her waist and guided her deftly onto the dance floor.

Even the extra glasses of champagne couldn't make Abigail forget that it was the first time he'd thought of dancing with her all evening. That knowledge kept her wooden in his clasp, and then, to her horror, she kicked

Blair's ankle sharply when another couple veered into their path. "I'm sorry," she muttered, feeling him draw in a painful breath.

"Not at all," he said, but he made no effort to conceal his relief as the music ended. "Shall we get the farewells out of the way?"

"I beg your pardon?"

"Say good night to the nice ladies and gentlemen," he gritted out, leading her toward their table. "You *can* manage that?"

"If I can't, I'm sure you'll take over." Pulling up a few feet from the table, she faced him squarely. "You don't have to hang over me like I'm somebody on parole. I'll meet you out in front if you want to get your car out of the garage."

"How long will you be?"

"Five minutes or so. I'd hate to give people the idea that I'm trying to bundle them home."

"Nobody will think that—the music will go on for another half-hour or so. Just tell them that—"

"Good Lord! I know what to tell them. You don't have to put words in my mouth." She paused when a wine waiter offered still more champagne.

"No, thank you," Blair told him, answering for both of them.

Abigail took a slow breath, mentally counting to five. She didn't plan to make a practice of getting tipsy, but at that moment she would liked to have chugalugged the entire bottle of champagne just to show Blair what she thought of his dictatorial ways. Still seething inwardly, she pulled away toward her table of dinner guests, saying to Blair over her shoulder, "I'll meet you at the car as soon as I can make my excuses."

"You're sure you're all right?"

"Just go!"

His jaw tightened ominously at her command but he turned and made his way out of the room.

Abigail spared just an instant to keep her gaze on his broad shoulders and then she turned unhappily to her task, knowing it wasn't cutting the party short that worried her, it was the drive to Jonas' which made her thoughts churn frantically.

When she slid onto the front seat beside Blair a little later, his opening remark did nothing to reassure her.

"I was just about to come and get you," he said grimly. "Especially after trying to convince a parking checker that I wasn't a permanent fixture in the loading zone."

"I did the best I could," Abigail said, shifting so that her long skirt wasn't wrinkled. "It took a while to make sure that everyone knew I was leaving. And why."

Blair's eyebrows climbed and he took advantage of a red traffic light to shoot a sideways look at her. "There was no reason to go into details."

She shrugged. "It wasn't hard. They all understood when I explained that I was going with you."

"Explained?"

"That's right. I told them I had to drive you back to Jonas' since you'd had a little too much champagne."

A silence followed her pronouncement, lasting until the blast of a horn from the car behind reminded Blair that the light had turned to green. He swore under his breath then and lost no time getting under way. "Thanks very much," he told Abigail when they were almost at the end of the next block. "I'd repay the compliment if I weren't leaving town tomorrow. Considering the reputation you've given me, it's just as well."

His words had brought a twinge of almost physical pain to her insides. "I didn't know you were going away," she said in a low tone.

"I finally heard that I passed my bar exams so it's time to follow up on some interviews. That part-time job with Jonas has been fine but now I need to get back on track in my field." He smiled wryly. "A different kind of caged birds."

"Jonas didn't mention you were just marking time at the clinic."

"He didn't know at the beginning and you haven't been around lately."

"Well, there were finals and moving off campus these last weekends."

"My good girl—nobody's blaming you." He sounded almost amused by her fervent defense.

"I'm *not* your good girl," she cut in hotly.

"You can say that again. More of a pint-sized pain in the neck. Tonight, at least."

"It's gratifying to know that I haven't completely ruined your life. Especially since you usually have to stop and think before you can remember my name."

"Just the first week or so," he said, accelerating when they finally reached the arterial heading north, which connected with the freeway. "After that, you left an indelible impression."

Abigail, remembering the way he'd disappear out the back of her uncle's house whenever she entered the front door, surmised that her imprint wasn't the kind wrapped in red velvet ribbon. Blair's casual approach had annoyed her from the beginning and she'd been more fractious than necessary the few times they'd been alone together. It had happened again at the party and probably the only result she'd garner from that was a blasting headache. She'd rubbed her temples, miserably aware that at least one of her brilliant deductions was already coming true.

"You look a little green," Blair commented, showing her that he knew what was going on beside him despite coping with solid traffic as they merged into the freeway north. "If you feel sick, for God's sake, say so. Now."

"I'm perfectly all right—" She broke off as he used the electric controls to lower the window at her side and let a rush of fresh air into the car. Before she could protest, she took a deep breath and discovered that the air *did* make her feel better. Her tense stomach muscles appreciated the diversion, although she hadn't been aware until that very moment that she was feeling queasy. She inhaled deeply, realizing that the final ignominy for the evening would be having her head held at the edge of the highway.

"Just lean back and rest until we get to Jonas' place," Blair was going on in a more kindly tone. "Once the traffic thins, the trip won't take long. And after a good night's sleep, you'll be fighting fit tomorrow. At least you didn't mix your drinks."

Abigail managed to nod. She couldn't have replied because her teeth were tightly clenched together to keep from grinding them in anger. My Lord! Next thing he'd be offering his handkerchief and probably would pin it to her coat sleeve to make sure she didn't lose it like a kindergartener.

Fortunately, there wasn't any more discussion after that and her stomach was feeling almost back to normal when they pulled into her uncle's drive a half-hour later.

She welcomed both the darkness and quiet as he turned off the ignition—reaching hastily for the door handle before Blair could come around to assist her. An earlier rain shower had dampened Jonas' curving front walk and she could still see the shiny leaves of the rhododendrons which were banked against the house. A thin cloud layer diffused the light of a harvest moon, but even with the overcast there was still enough illumination so that a helping hand wasn't necessary. When they reached the front step, Abigail suddenly found it vital to search for her key and Blair was forced to hover.

He let her spend a perceptible interval groping for it before he sighed and pulled his own key from his pocket. "This might save some time," he said dryly, inserting it in the lock and opening the door.

If Abigail had used her common sense she would simply have nodded and thanked him before going on into the house. However, she was still smarting from his officious demeanor in the car, so she tilted her chin and said sarcastically, "Of course—I should have known.

You've made yourself at home since you've been working here, haven't you?"

"What exactly is that supposed to mean?"

"Just that my uncle has a reputation as a softhearted man, so it's easy to take advantage of him. I'm sure you've found that out."

"Would you like to count the silver before I leave?"

"That shouldn't be necessary." She let her glance run dismissingly over his still figure. "You wouldn't have tried anything so obvious."

"Thanks very much."

"If you'd like, though, I could take your key and give it to him in the morning." She kept her tone uncaring. "Since you won't be needing it anymore."

"No, thanks. I'll give it to him myself. That way, I'll know for sure it's delivered. Now, you'd better get some sleep." He smiled unpleasantly. "If you need help finding the bed, I can oblige. . . ." As her hand came up fast, he caught it in an iron grip before she could do any damage. "My God, you *are* asking for trouble."

His words hit like chips of ice but she didn't waver in her defiance. "That's a fine way to talk—after you've done and said everything possible to insult me. All night long."

"I thought I'd done you a favor."

"Some favor. Making me listen to a lecture most of the way home and sounding off like a temperance groupie just because I had a little too much champagne."

"Keep your voice down. Unless you want to wake Jonas up in the middle of the night."

His rebuke made Abigail even more annoyed and she

clenched her fists helplessly at her side. "*Must* you keep telling me what to do?"

"Only because of your 'weakened condition,' " he gibed. "Once you get back in shape, you'll be able to handle anything."

"At least I'm able to take care of you—if that's what you had in mind."

His thick eyebrows went up at her boast. "With one hand tied behind you? Or maybe two?"

"I don't know what you're talking about. . . ."

"Let me show you." He caught her wrists and pulled them behind her with deceptive ease as he continued conversationally, "I'd hate to think that I'd taken advantage, since you're slightly sozzled. On the other hand, somebody should have told you a long time ago that you can't dish out insults without expecting to get paid back in kind. And you can stop struggling because it won't do any good."

Abigail had already discovered that. His clasp felt like steel on her wrists and his free hand wasn't gentle as it clamped onto her shoulder. He'd pulled her so close that she was aware of every inch of his muscular strength through the thin fabric of her evening blouse and skirt. The intimacy had an unexpected effect on her and it was as much of an effort to control her breathing as her inclination to relax against that broad chest. Her inner struggle left her words thin and tremulous. "If you don't get your hands off me I'll . . . I'll . . ."

"You'll what?" he asked derisively and then shoved her at arm's length to avoid her knee as she brought it up between them.

His sudden jerk backward pulled her off guard and unable to do any more damage along that line, even when Blair once more molded her body against his. "Don't try that again," he warned through clenched teeth. "Little girls are apt to get more than they bargained for with that kind of tactic."

"That's not what they told us in my self-defense class," she said, glad that she'd at least gotten his attention. "Just let go of me and maybe I'll forget to mention this to Jonas in the morning."

"That's got me quaking in my shoes," he told her with a snort of laughter. "Well, here's something really to complain about."

The last word was barely uttered before his mouth came down on hers in a punishing kiss. Abby tried to draw back, gasping in protest, but the brief parting of her lips was all Blair needed to harden his own assault. His devastating probing and plundering completely undermined her resistance until his clasp on her shoulders was all that kept her from sinking onto the cold concrete of the porch.

Long afterward, she realized that she should have slapped him or kicked him or bitten him or something— when he finally raised his head. Instead, like a simpleton, she dropped her head onto his shoulder as she tried to get her breathing into a semblance of normalcy and the stiffening back into her knees.

Evidently her dazed condition must have gotten through to the man she was clutching with such desperation because there was a rough note in his voice as he asked, "Abby? Are you all right?"

By then she was aware that the heartbeat in his chest was thumping along in regular fashion. Certainly it wasn't off on a tear the way her own was behaving. Which showed that the kiss hadn't put him in a pelter. Far from it! He was probably enjoying the knowledge that she was a shapeless blob hanging on to his shirtfront.

Abby closed her eyes for an instant and then made a superhuman effort to pull herself together. She managed to say, "Of course I'm all right. Good Lord, you don't think such juvenile behavior would throw me, do you?" She straightened and made a production out of massaging the muscles at the back of her neck that had been painfully stretched as she'd struggled against that first punishing kiss. "Maybe if I'd not had quite so much champagne," she said, keeping her voice light and uncaring, "the net result wouldn't have been so bad. As it was . . ." She let her words trail off deliberately.

There was a brief silence before he picked up the cue. "As it was?" he prompted.

"I just feel nauseated." Even in the dim moonlight, she could see the dark color rising to his cheekbones and she felt a surge of triumph. "So unless you have any more bright ideas—I'd like to go to bed. You'll forgive me if I don't say thanks for the ride home or anything else."

He let his hand fall from her waist but that was the only indication that her sarcasm had registered. "I really didn't expect it. And you'll understand if I don't say thanks for the party—or anything else."

It was the final touch for the evening as far as Abby was concerned. The headache she'd been trying to ignore all the way home started battering against her temples and the nausea that before had been only a figment of her imagination suddenly made her stomach muscles tighten.

She *did* retain enough presence of mind to keep from blurting out her predicament, but her agonized expression must have told him the whole story as she bolted for her bedroom, without another word.

The night which followed was a horror of its own. When she finally thought she could manage a cup of tea early the next morning, she found Jonas alone in the kitchen with the news that Blair had said good-bye a few minutes earlier.

It was strange how the experience had stayed crystal clear in her mind during the months that followed. She'd been fortunate in finding a job in fashion advertising which was challenging and promised a topflight salary when she'd garnered enough experience. She was lucky in her co-workers and discovered there were any number of men who obviously enjoyed her company. But even a glimpse of a tall, dark-haired stranger was enough to make her catch her breath, bringing back memories of that last devastating encounter with Blair Morley. And now, realizing that she was expected to meet him again made the fantasy world become reality. It wasn't surprising that she quaked inwardly. When she finally got around to putting the coffee mugs on a tray, their contents had gone completely lukewarm. Jonas came out into the kitchen then to see what had happened.

"Something wrong?" he asked with a puzzled frown.

"Wrong?" She made an obvious effort to join the world again. "No, of course not. Everything's ready . . ." Her voice faltered as she hefted the mugs and then put them back on the counter. "I'm sorry." She shook her head as if to clear it. "I'll make some more coffee. It won't take a minute."

"This'll do fine," Jonas said gallantly as he took a mug and gestured her ahead of him out to the living room. "If I had the chance of a Bermuda vacation, I'd be daydreaming, too. Unless you're worrying about going there during the hurricane season." He grinned and ruffled her hair. "You may find that you have a more exciting stay than you planned. Any last wills and testaments that need to be made?"

She smiled in response as she perched on the edge of his chair. "That depends. Currently, you'll inherit my unpaid car loan, my Norfolk pine . . ."

"The one that's dropping its needles all over the floor?"

She nodded. "None other. Oh, and you also get my unfinished macrame wall divider. How's that for generosity?"

Jonas groaned feelingly. "I should have known. Is it any use asking you to try Hawaii or someplace closer to home?"

"You might just be able to do it," Abby said, only half-joking. The prospect of meeting Blair again might be worth a change of plans.

Her uncle clearly didn't take her seriously. "I wish I had some time for a trip now. The fall season has always been the nicest time to travel so far as I'm concerned. Incidentally, Blair will try to meet you at the airport there. If he can't make it, he'll come around to your hotel to pick up that report I mentioned."

Abigail wanted to ask if Blair had added any scathing comments about her coming, but she didn't have the nerve. Besides, he wasn't apt to mention that long-ago night any more than she was. Especially since he hadn't said anything about it at the time.

"I'll deliver your report one way or another," she told Jonas. "Probably the easiest way would be to leave it at the reception desk at the hotel—then Blair can pick it up whenever it's convenient for him."

"I'd rather you delivered it personally. I've put a lot of time into those pages and I'd hate to have them go astray at this point," Jonas said, sounding sterner than usual. "Besides, I think Blair would be a little offended if you tried anything like that."

"Probably he'd be tickled pink. By now he must have a steady girlfriend or a long list in his black book."

"That may be, but he said that he'd find time to fit you in." Jonas saw Abigail's eyebrows arch and then come together in a threatening line. "I'm sure that he didn't mean that the way it sounded," he went on, hoping to placate her.

"Fit me in, will he? I can tell he hasn't changed one bit—even after all these months. Well, he'll find that two can play at that game and I've learned a few more rules by now."

"That sounds a little ominous. What happened between you two? Nothing serious, I hope."

Jonas' words showed that he didn't like the trend of her conversation, even though the substance was beyond him. Abigail shook her head and gave him an impulsive hug. "Of course not. I'll put your report right in Blair's hands if that's what you want."

"Good." Jonas settled back in his chair when Abby straightened again. "Then I won't have to worry about you."

"Heavens, no." She had a thoughtful expression on her face as she continued slowly, "*I'll* be just fine."

Jonas was watching her steadily. "Should I keep my fingers crossed for Blair?"

Abigail's soft lips quirked in amusement. "It wouldn't hurt. After all, it is the stormy season down there."

"I suppose you're too old to be told to behave yourself?"

"I'll be a perfect lady. Save your warnings for Blair."

"Storm warnings?"

"You could call it that."

He shook his head, chuckling. "I'll wait for the final weather report. But, Abby, my love . . ."

She looked at him inquiringly.

"Don't get hurt," he said, his voice carefully level.

"Hurricanes have been flirting with Bermuda for years, but they usually just skirt the edge of the islands." Her hands went out in a graceful gesture, as if downplaying his concern. "I'll be fine. If worse comes to worst, I'll stay in my hotel room and pull the covers over my head."

"Dear heaven, that would be the worst possible thing. I wouldn't recommend the bedroom."

"What's wrong with the bedroom in a hurricane?" she asked, alarmed.

"Who's talking about hurricanes?" Jonas said with some amusement. "Just make sure that all the storm centers stay offshore, and avoid any manmade disasters."

Chapter Two

Bermuda hadn't changed very much since the time she'd last seen it. Abigail decided that as the plane completed its final approach to the long runway at Kindley Field and settled onto the ground with hardly a jarring note.

The smooth landing was in keeping with her first view of land a few minutes before. Suddenly rising out of the gray-green waters of the Atlantic, the islands provided a mélange of colors so bright and beautiful that they seemed wonderfully unreal.

. She could understand how one of the island's earliest explorers—Admiral Sir George Somers—instructed that his heart be left in Bermuda after his death in 1610, although his body was taken back to England for a hero's burial. The natural beauty of the colony had been enchanting residents ever since.

The surge of warm, humid air that greeted Abby as

she stepped out of the plane brought back other memories; it wasn't the first time she'd boarded a jet in one season and emerged into another. In this case, the turning leaves on the trees and the temperature at home had shown tinges of fall, but the Bermuda day turned the calendar back; summer was lingering there with a vengeance. Even as she smiled at the stewardess who was standing by the bottom of the stairs, Abby was well aware that her coral gabardine suit which had seemed so sensible hours before was already feeling like a parka and the beige coat over her arm wouldn't be taken out of the closet unless a rain shower threatened.

Surreptitiously she blotted her forehead with the back of her hand as she trailed into the terminal to retrieve her luggage. She'd managed a last-minute application of lipstick and powder before they'd landed so that she'd look halfway decent but she had a suspicion that the humidity was going to make a mockery of her efforts. Blair would just have to take her as she came!

Ten minutes later as she stood in lonely splendor in a corner of the terminal with her bags at her side, she decided that it didn't really matter what she looked like just then because Blair Morley wasn't going to take her at all. Obviously he hadn't managed to fit her arrival into his damned schedule.

She frowned as she surveyed the rapidly emptying waiting room, wondering if she'd lingered so long that all the taxis would have disappeared from the rank outside. One thing was for sure, she'd never find out if she continued to skulk in the corner like a piece of unwanted baggage. She reached down to grasp the handle of her heaviest bag, hoping that her shoulder purse wouldn't catapult to the floor in the maneuver. It didn't—it waited until she bent to pick up the other bag, and thus necessitated putting everything down again before starting over.

Halfway through the process, she decided that she probably should leave a message with the airline ticket desk—in the dim possibility that Blair might call or arrive later. She'd say that she'd gone into Hamilton and neglect to mention the name of her hotel. That way, she could call him when *she* found it convenient to get in touch.

She was pleased at even such a childish chance to score, because by then her gabardine suit jacket was clinging to her shoulders like a second skin and the tie on her silk blouse felt like a noose.

She shoved her bags against the wall, trusting that any potential luggage thieves wouldn't be working in the heat of the afternoon. Besides, the only people around were a couple of immigration officials huddled with their customs counterparts. As Abby approached the ticket counter of the airline on which she'd arrived, two male air crew in shirtsleeves, each carrying a scuffed leather bag, headed toward the glass terminal doors which led out to the taxi rank and parking area.

The attractive young lady behind the ticket counter was carrying on an animated telephone conversation as Abigail drew up in front of her. She held up a finger, indicating that she wouldn't be much longer, and Abby nodded. Finally the conversation came to an end with something that sounded like "I'll see you at seven, then—by the pool." The girl turned a smiling face as she put down the receiver. "Yes, miss? Is there something I can help you with?"

"I'd like to leave a message, please," Abby said in a businesslike tone. "I was expecting to be met, but evidently the gentleman has been held up. If Blair Morley calls . . ." Her words trailed off as she saw a horrified expression come over the ticket agent's face. "What's wrong?" Abby asked, frowning.

"Are you . . . are you Miss Trent?" the other queried, pulling a folded note from a clipboard. "Flight 601?"

"Why, yes."

"I'm terribly sorry," the girl said, shoving the paper across the counter as if it singed her fingers. "I meant to have you paged as soon as the flight arrived, but something came up." She shot a guilty glance toward the telephone.

"I see." Abby nodded, aware that the same something was going to come up again by the pool at seven. She turned away from the counter and opened the note. Although she had a very good idea of its contents, her knuckles went white as she read the message. "Mr. Morley has been detained and he won't be able to meet your plane. He'll be in touch with you at your hotel tomorrow or the next day."

"Is everything all right?"

Abigail looked up to find the ticket girl staring at her anxiously. "Yes. Yes, of course," she replied, her voice gaining strength on her second attempt to get the words out. "Why?"

"Nothing. You'd just gone so pale. Would you like to lie down for a few minutes?"

"No, thanks." Abby's voice was rueful. "When I lie down I hope it will be for about ten hours. Bermuda's a long way from the west coast and the clock's catching up with me."

The girl looked relieved. "I can understand that. Do you have a hotel reservation?"

Abby nodded. "All I need right now is a taxi."

"I can help with that, too." The girl gestured toward an elderly black man who was laughing with another man by the wide glass doors of the terminal. "Lem— come and get to work, man. This lady wants a taxi."

"My bags are over by the wall," Abby began, remembering suddenly.

"Don't worry, I'll take care of them, miss. Just point them out and we'll be on our way," the driver said with a smile, as he ambled over to the counter.

After she slid onto the backseat of his small taxi and saw her bags stored safely in the trunk, Abigail gave him the name of her hotel. She relaxed against the seat then and watched as he drove out the winding airport road, turning onto the main thoroughfare toward Hamilton a few minutes later.

"I s'pose this weather seems hot if you're not used to it," the man said amiably over his shoulder as he passed two moped riders and accelerated to the twenty-mile-per-hour speed limit on the narrow two-lane road. "Once you get in the air conditioning of your hotel, it'll be more comfortable. Even that won't help this humidity, though," he admitted, pulling out a handkerchief and mopping the back of his neck.

"Maybe that will get better in a day or so." Abby was glad that she had some excuse for her drawn expression, which hadn't gone unnoticed by any of the natives. Blair's casual message had been like a dash of cold water on her spirits, but even that hadn't been able to counteract the island's soggy humidity. She pulled out her own handkerchief and blotted her cheeks. "I didn't expect this in September."

"We do," the driver said, catching her glance briefly in the rear-vision mirror. "It's hurricane season."

"Oh, Lord . . ."

"You don't have to worry these days," he said hurriedly. "All the weather is served up to us on a plate by the government folks. And there's plenty of warning, so there's no reason for it to spoil your holiday. Maybe a little inconvenience, but nothing serious."

"You mean there actually *is* a hurricane coming?" Abby said, her voice rising.

"Not right away. Last I heard on the radio, one's playing around down in the Caribbean and they're still not sure where it's headed. Maybe it'll brush the Bahamas and then out into the Atlantic. That's the usual way."

"I see." Abigail bit her lip and then relaxed again against the worn vinyl seat of the car. She turned to stare out at the pleasure craft moored in the quiet waters of Flatts Inlet as the taxi went over the stone bridge and passed the local aquarium with its usual quota of tour buses in the parking lot. Brilliant oleanders grew luxuriantly on either side of the roadway, interspersed with coral block fences a little later on and even more rampantly growing morning glories with bright blue blossoms. As the car progressed along the North Shore Road, Abby's attention focused on the right side, where the swelling waters of the Atlantic surged against the powdered coral beaches and rocky elevations. The houses became more plentiful as they approached Bermuda's capital, and green grass lawns provided an attractive contrast to pastel shades which Bermudans had chosen for their residences. There were pinks and blues, yellows and greens in all sizes and degrees of affluence, but they had one thing in common: chalk-white, identically styled roofs which caught the vital drops of rain because the island had no other supply of fresh water.

The whine of mopeds increased as traffic thickened when the taxi reached the outskirts of Hamilton. Abigail smiled at the sight of elderly men in business jackets, ties, and Bermuda shorts whipping along on their motorbikes. They all wore safety helmets, as did women riders outfitted in high heels, who were calmly carrying home groceries, as well.

"It's not like it used to be," Abby's taximan said ruefully as two cyclists risked a collision with a local bus when they didn't lessen their speed at a congested intersection. "Those things are inventions of the devil."

"It must have been quieter when they just had regular bikes," Abby agreed. "And quieter still before they allowed cars on the island. When did all that change?"

"Nineteen forty-six. I'm not so sure it was a good idea," the driver said, sighing as he missed a traffic light because of congestion as they approached Hamilton's popular Front Street, where tourists lined the sidewalks and lingered to shop for duty-free bargains at the famous stores. The crowds of shoppers made the city center look more like Broadway on New Year's Eve than an island hide- away.

"I hope it will be less crowded at the hotel," she ventured as the taximan managed to pull around a horse- drawn sightseeing carriage and finally get through the intersection.

"I wouldn't count on it. There's a big convention there. Dentists."

Abby's mouth dropped open. If there were anything guaranteed to kill romantic overtones on an island vacation, it was a hotel crammed to the rafters with dentists. "You mean Bermuda dentists?" she asked hope- fully as they drove down a road near the water.

"No, ma'am. American dentists. They came in by charter planes yesterday. There's not an extra hotel room to be had all week."

"Great," she said bitterly, as hopes of walks along quiet beaches while communing with nature died aborning.

"You have a reservation where you're going?" he wanted to know.

"I certainly hope so. If not"—she managed a crooked smile—"you'll have to take me back to the airport."

He shook his head. "No point in that. I hear there aren't any plane reservations to be had. The weather report's responsible."

"You mean . . . the threat of that hurricane?" She

leaned forward and put her forearms on the back of the front seat to carry on the conversation more easily. "But you said that nobody even knows if there's going to be one!"

"That's right. But lots of folks don't want to take any chances. Even the captains of those cruise liners in the harbor are anchored out in midstream. They won't stick around if there's any chance of storm damage."

"What do they do?"

"Go out to sea." He shook his head dolefully as he slowed to turn in a curving drive in front of a luxurious waterfront hotel. "Not that I'd want to ship out when there was heavy weather on the horizon. I'll take my chances on dry land. One good thing about a hurricane in the offing—it'll sure clear out the crowds." As he braked in front of the hotel entrance, he turned off the ignition and added, "One way or another."

It was a dubious distinction for a vacation, Abby reflected as she got out of the cab. A little later, when she'd paid her fare and made sure that her bags were transferred to the doorman, the sight of people with convention badges and very white teeth who were registering at the front desk sent another surge of gloom through her.

She noted the clerks were exhibiting an independence and aloofness that only a sold-out hotel brings and hoped that she didn't end up in a closet overlooking the parking lot. Next time I'll try Timbuktu, she decided as she dodged a golf bag slithering off a load of luggage when a bellman tried to pile it too high. She wasn't surprised to see several other golf bags piled in the corner.

Dentists had to do something to fill up weekends while their patients got toothaches and lost fillings. She was still scowling over that when she reached the registration desk and clerk said, "Yes, miss?"

"My name is Trent. I have a reservation," she announced, all set to fight.

The man thumbed through a list and then slid a card onto the counter in front of her. "Yes, Miss Trent. Will you register, please. We have an oceanfront room for you—one of our nicer ones." He snapped his fingers to get the attention of a bellman. "Miss Trent's luggage. Room 214." Turning back to Abigail, he smiled and said, "Enjoy your stay. If there's anything we can do to make it more pleasant, don't hesitate to let us know."

"Thank you," Abby managed feebly. "I'm sure everything will be just fine."

A few minutes later, when she'd followed the bellman down a charming garden walk to one of the hotel's newer wings overlooking the harbor and a sparkling saltwater swimming pool, she realized that "fine" was an understatement. Her room was immaculate with spanking white cotton spreads on the twin beds and a vibrant blue rug on the floor. The same blue tone was picked up on the vinyl pads of the iron lounge and chair on her balcony, which overlooked the pool and the picturesque inner Hamilton harbor.

"Will there be anything else, miss?"

The bellman's polite query brought Abby back into the room. "No, thank you," she said, managing to find the dollar bills she'd tucked in her jacket for specifically that purpose.

He nodded cheerfully and was at the hall door when he came face to face with a beautiful, tall brunette in a crisp white linen coatdress. She made an especially attractive picture, since she was carrying a vase filled with red carnations.

"They told me Miss Trent had just arrived," she said in a distinctly British accent. And then, as she peered around the bellman to note Abby, her smile beamed a welcome. She brushed her shoulder-length black hair away from her face with her free hand and offered her the bouquet with a graceful gesture. "I did so want to have these here when you arrived. Now I'll have to confess to Blair that I've spoiled everything." She turned to raise a reproving eyebrow at the bellman, still lingering nearby, and it was enough to make him quickly close the door behind him. Then she turned back to Abby and said, "The help these days! Not the way things used to be, mind you."

Abby could have told her that staffing difficulties weren't a problem in her life-style, but she refrained, saying only, "What a lovely bouquet," as she put the flowers on the dressing table. "I don't see a card on it."

The other woman grimaced. "My fault again. You'd never think I had enough sense to assist Blair in his work, would you? By the way, I'm Maida Collins."

She hesitated perceptibly and Abigail had the feeling that the other woman expected more of a response than her own slightly puzzled expression.

Maida didn't let the silence lengthen between them. "I thought perhaps Blair might have mentioned me when he wrote. Although I'm really not surprised. He's such a clam—I never knew what he was thinking when I first started working for him. Of course, now"—she smoothed the snugly fitting skirt at her hipline with an almost sensual gesture—"now it's a little different. Have you known him long?"

The last words were tossed out as if they really didn't matter. Ordinarily Abby would have admitted, "I haven't seen him in ages," but Maida's staking her claim was hardly diplomatic. Not that the woman had any reason to fear competition, Abby thought even as she decided to make a few waves of her own. "He's an old friend of the family. It was sweet of him to send flowers—just like old times."

Maida's pale blue eyes narrowed, but only momentarily. "Well, then I'll tell Blair that you're nicely settled in and that you approved of the carnations I selected."

Abby's smile stayed firmly in place. "They're one of my favorite flowers," she said, following the brunette to the hall doorway and reaching for the knob. "It's been lovely meeting you. Probably we'll be seeing each other again."

"Bound to." Maida's glance ran over her quickly. "Once you get some rest, this weather won't seem so devastating and you'll be all set for tours around the island. The hotel social desk can arrange them, but if there's anything Blair or I can do . . ."

"You've done more than enough." That much, at least, was true, Abby thought, baring her teeth politely.

"It was a pleasure." The brunette waggled her fingers in a charming gesture of farewell. "Keep in touch."

"I'll do that, Miss Collins."

The woman lingered on the threshold. "Actually, it's Mrs. Collins."

Abby's heartbeat bounded inexplicably. "Oh?"

"I've been a widow for over a year." Maida's lovely features took on a look of fortitude. Only a fiend would suspect that the expression had been thoroughly rehearsed, Abby thought. If Blair fell for that act, he deserved all he was undoubtedly getting.

She watched surreptitiously as Maida walked down the hall toward the stairs. Each purposeful step showed Blair's assistant or secretary or whatever was equally glad the "welcome" visit was over.

Abby closed the door and leaned against it for an instant, suddenly feeling as unwanted as the flotsam which edged the beaches on the North Shore Road during her drive to Hamilton. She wandered over to the dressing table and fingered one of the carnations, subduing an urge to dump the entire bouquet in the wastebasket. The least she could do was give it to one of the maids later so somebody could get enjoyment from the flowers. In the meantime, she'd have a swim in that saltwater pool below her balcony and see if that would help her mood.

It was probably the most sensible thing she'd done since leaving home. The sparkling free-form pool in its setting of palms and pink stucco looked like something from a gorgeous travel poster. When Abby slipped into the cool water, the rays of the late-afternoon sun and even the heavy humidity could be ignored.

Fortunately, the improving trend continued. After

she emerged, dripping, a little later, a tall fair-haired man in his late twenties made a point of walking over to courteously offer a towel from the stack nearby. He was a member of a British charter air crew on layover and introduced himself as Ian Woodbourne. He was polite and tentative rather than pushy about offering to show her some of the more attractive beaches on the south shore if she preferred surf to swimming pools. "As a matter of fact, I thought I'd take the hotel launch to Warwick in the morning if I get up in time," he said casually. "There's a good beach club over there."

"Can we use it?" Abby wanted to know as she pulled a terry shift over her flowered jersey swimsuit for the walk back to her room.

"No problem about that," Ian said, squinting slightly against the sunshine. "Reciprocal hotel rights and all that." He put investigative fingers up to test the skin on his forehead, which was turning decidedly pink. "Unless I've overdone things today. Even so, I'd be glad to sit in the shade of a palm tree and watch you."

"Get parboiled?" Abby threw him a friendly grin. "I have to take it slow, too. Otherwise, I'll resemble those Bermuda fish that look like pumpkins."

"Not to worry. I think you'd look good no matter what. And you don't have to decide now. You can let me know at breakfast. We all congregate in the hotel dining room at the same time, so I'll keep an eye out for you. If we miss connections, I'll ring you later. Unless you'd rather make up your mind over dinner with me?" He eyed her thoughtfully.

"Let's wait until breakfast, thanks. Right now, I'm

still on the wrong time zone and I may not even make it to dinner." She pushed her pink beach towel into a convenient receptacle nearby and slipped on a pair of rubber thongs. "See you later."

"You can count on that," Ian said with a fervor which did wonders for her spirits.

Once back in her room, Abby enjoyed a shower and took time to rinse out her swimsuit before hanging it on the shower rail to dry. Then she unpacked a silk jacquard chemise, which was both flattering and still wrinkle-free, for dinner in the hotel's coffee shop off the lobby. After tossing a sweater around her shoulders, she picked up Jonas' report and slipped it under her arm along with a magazine to read during the meal. When she'd finished dinner, she'd leave the report at the front desk, where Blair could pick it up at his convenience. That would show him that she had no intention of being at his beck and call during her short vacation. At the same time, it would spare her any more condescending visits from his secretary, who bequeathed bouquets like royalty granting favors.

Abby let herself out a side door for the short walk up the winding concrete track to the main building. The sun was at horizon level by then and the towering palms and thick shrubbery cast long shadows over the manicured lawns on either side. A flash of color to her right made her pause, frowning, and then her forehead smoothed as she identified a young cat crouching at the base of a palm tree. He was intent on some small prey he was holding captive with a front paw, and if the grass hadn't been recently watered, Abby would have detoured by for a closer look. Marmalade cats were favorites of hers and this one was an appealing size— probably just under a year, with all the curiosity of a kitten and the unquenchable spirit of approaching manhood. He was mainly orange stripes, but a few black markings along his sides provided additional color. Abby's presence on the sidewalk eventually attracted his attention, but he took care to keep his paw on his quarry while he subjected her to an unblinking stare.

"You'd do better hunting at the kitchen door," Abby advised him solemnly. "Unless you're on the European plan while you're here." As the cat continued to stare back at her, Abby's glance took in his streamlined shape. A little too streamlined at the ribs, she decided. "I'll try to save something from dinner if you're still around by then."

The memory of that promise prompted her to order prawns for dinner when she'd only planned on some soup or a small sandwich. That meant eating her way through a bowl of soup, the salad, and a generous dessert that went with the dinner entrée just so she could manage to stow three prawns in a paper napkin afterward. She shook her head ruefully as she wrapped them up. Obviously the cat would have to fend for himself after this or she'd do more harm than good. Both to his scrounging talents and her waistline.

It was hard to ignore the hotel clerk's raised eyebrows when she later had to put the fishy-smelling napkin on the marble counter so that she could arrange for a safe-deposit box to house Jonas' report. That came about after the dignified man at the reception desk—who'd obviously never carried *anything* in a paper napkin in his life—asserted that the hotel couldn't be responsible for a valuable report left at the main desk. He did condescend to leave a message so that Blair would know it was in a safe-deposit box on the premises.

Considering Ian's invitation and the errands she'd planned, Blair might find it was a while before she could fit him into *her* social schedule. That prospect was so pleasing that Abby signed the safe-deposit card with a flourish and swept up her box key along with her slightly greasy napkin, once the report was safely stowed away.

Darkness had fallen by the time she emerged from the main building, and the slight breeze rustling the palm fronds along the walk made her glad that she wore her sweater over her shoulders. The temperature had fallen but the humidity hadn't lessened appreciably even in the early evening. Abby didn't dwell on it; the lights of the homes dotting the islets just beyond Hamilton harbor and the navigation lights on the ferries surging through the black water provided such a lovely vista that she forgot about minor annoyances.

The deserted pathway and curtained windows of the guest rooms in the main wing alongside made her feel that she was the only person registered in the hotel. Apparently most Bermuda visitors weren't wasting any of their holiday time in their rooms at the shank of the evening. Instead they were in the big bar off the lobby, and still more were lined up trying to get tickets for a nightclub show featuring a chorus line that rivaled Las Vegas for nonexistent costumes. But all that activity seemed part of another world and the only sounds Abigail heard as she went toward her room were the noise of her heels on the concrete walk, the rustling of the trees in the occasional stirring of wind, and an intermittent squeak like a rusty hinge, which must have come from one of those winged insects the cat was pursuing earlier.

That made her aware of the prawn-filled napkin still clutched in her hand. She was foolish not to have remembered that darkness would have fallen during dinner and even orange-striped cats weren't highly visible under the garden lights, which were at a bare minimum; just enough to mark the edges of the walk, a spotlight at the entrance doors of the various buildings, and, still ahead, a muted lighting at the saltwater pool.

Unfortunately, the young tomcat wasn't in any of those lighted areas, which left only the putting green, dark and uninviting behind a low privet hedge to her left, unless she wanted to start scouring the grounds.

She disregarded that possibility immediately; it was bad enough to skirt around the edge of the hedge, ignoring the prickly bits which caught her skirt in the maneuver and the damp grass which squished under her shoes. "Here kitty . . . kitty . . . kitty," she coaxed in an undertone. "Want to eat, kitty?" she added as she impulsively opened the napkin so that the prawn odor could waft onto the night air.

She stood quietly waiting for a response, shifting her feet and trying to find some part of the putting green which hadn't been inundated by the gardening crew. At least none of the guests in the wing which overlooked the area had come storming onto their balconies wondering what idiot was adrift.

And she *was* an idiot, she told herself scornfully as she waited a full minute longer without success. The cat was probably sleeping off his earlier dinner on a lounger down by the swimming pool and could care less that he had a self-appointed welfare worker just yards away.

The hell with it! she decided, and started to skirt the ornamental pool which provided a scenic boundary to the putting green in the daylight but looked like a blob of black ink just then. At its scalloped concrete edge, Abigail hesitated and looked down at the prawns in her hand. She couldn't very well put them in the wastebasket in her room; the only alternatives were to leave them in a discreet spot on the grounds or walk around to the pier at the front of the hotel. That meant going through the lobby again just to toss the damned things into the briny. A fugitive brainstorm for dumping them in a receptacle at the saltwater pool was squashed aborning. She'd just lay them in a neat pile on the edge of the ornamental pool by her feet and hope to heaven that they'd be gone by daylight. The possibility that she was courting an inquisitive rat was pushed firmly to the back of her mind as she knelt to dispose of the prawns. A rustling nearby made her look over her shoulder and whisper, "Kitty?" hopefully. Another rustling, considerably more forceful, brought her to her feet in a jerky movement. It was instinct rather than knowledge which made her take a step toward the path. Anything— anything—to get out of the deep shadows and back into civilization again.

She gasped when a broad figure loomed up from the thick shrubbery. As his arms came out to clutch her, she opened her mouth to scream. Then a tough palm slapped across her face and sharp pain seared her as cruel fingers tightened on her skin. Abruptly the intruder gave her a rough shove with his other hand, sending her to the ground, still clawing to fight back.

When her head slammed onto the concrete edge of the pool, her mounting shriek of terror was her last conscious thought before another darkness—as still and black as the Bermuda night around her—shrouded her motionless figure.

Chapter Three

Abigail's next coherent thoughts came in painful, laborious steps. Her mind tried to emerge from the shadows, but at first the effort was too monumental. Only the certainty that she was profoundly uncomfortable finally made her decide to find out why.

It didn't take long; her eyes fluttered open as a deluge of cold water splashed over her face, and since the soggy feeling went right down to her waist, she deduced it wasn't her first inundation.

Determined that there wouldn't be another one, she struggled to sit upright, but found a strong arm was holding her down. That triggered memories of the shadowy figure, and she opened her mouth to scream again, only to get another handful of water in the face.

"Stop that!" she managed to gasp, and tried to scramble away from the dark figure crouching beside her.

Her sudden movement caught him unawares, and she

thought she'd gotten free until a wet hand clutched her ankle as she took the first step.

"Let go of me!" she repeated frantically, kicking to get free.

"Abigail! For God's sake, simmer down!" The man leaned forward, obviously trying to get a good look at her in the dim light by the pool. "It is *you*, isn't it?"

That deep voice brought back memories that were as painful as her throbbing head. "Blair?" she asked faintly, still crouched like a runner on the starting blocks as she peered toward his concerned face. Then her voice rose in disbelief. "I can't believe it. First you almost kill me, and now you try to drown me."

"What in the devil are you talking about? You'd still be flat out by this pool if I hadn't heard a commotion and come to investigate. And I'm sorry about the water—but I was just trying to bring you around." He paused and sniffed audibly. "Lord! You smell like a fish factory. They must not clean that pool very often. It's even on your hands," he announced as he helped her get to her feet.

Abigail's mind was clear enough then that she murmured, "That came from the prawns."

"What did you say?"

"Never mind." She wrinkled her nose as a whiff of fish-pond water wafted up from her clinging dress. "Yuk! It's like something the tide brought in."

"Prawns?" Blair gave her a wary look as his arm steadied her by his side. "You're still groggy. There may be some carp in there, but that's all."

"I'm talking about the prawns for the cat."

"What cat?"

"The one I couldn't find." She pulled to a stop at the edge of the path. "Where are you taking me?"

"To your room, of course. Once you get to bed, I'll call a doctor. Now what's the matter?"

"My key. My purse." She was rubbing her forehead to try and think. "I had it in the same hand as the napkin."

"What napkin?"

"The one with the prawns."

"For the nonexistent cat," he finished for her. "My God!"

"Well, he was there before dinner."

"I'm sure he was," he said, hastily trying another tack. "Never mind, I'll ask the maid about him when I try to find a passkey for your room."

"But I want my purse," she protested, pulling back toward the pool. "And what happened to my magazine?"

"Maybe your cat wanted some reading matter. Who gives a damn about that?" Blair said impatiently as he trailed her. "I'll buy you another magazine. Right now, I want to get to a telephone and let Security know that some crazy is running around the grounds."

"There he is! Right over there!" Abigail pointed a shaky finger toward the base of the palm, and then winced as Blair yanked her roughly back toward the lighted path. "You're hurting me," she whimpered.

"Sorry." He loosened his grip as his glance swept the pool area. "I don't see anybody."

She gestured toward the shadowy outline of the palm tree. "He was searching for another prawn."

He frowned at her. "You must have gotten a worse

crack on the head than I thought." Then his voice rose as he caught a glimpse of orange scuttling along the hedge out of sight. "My God! There really *is* a cat!"

She let out an exasperated snort. "Of course there is. What did you think I was talking about? That's why I was there in the first place—putting down prawns for him. But then somebody loomed up out of the shrubbery and knocked me down."

"He must have stepped on the cat in the middle of things, because there was a screech that could have been heard in Staten Island," Blair told her. "I was coming along the path just then and decided to investigate."

"Thank heavens you did!"

"You can say that again." As he felt a tremor go through her slender body, he propelled her toward the path. "If you don't get out of those wet clothes, you'll be suffering from more than a lump on the head."

"I know," she said, but she lingered to look over her shoulder. "Wait a second—there by the hedge. Is that my purse?"

Blair's glance followed where she was pointing. "It could be," he agreed. "I'll check. In the meantime . . ."

"I'll wait in the middle of the path," she said meekly.

He nodded and pointed her in the proper direction. "Better still—go stand by the building under that spotlight. Are you missing anything else?"

"Not that I can think of," she told him, remembering that Jonas' report was in the safe-deposit box. There was plenty of time to tell him about that later, she rationalized.

Barely two or three minutes passed before he rejoined

her, holding out her damp purse as he approached. "It's a little soggy from the grass but it looks as if everything's still there. Even your money and room key. The only thing that's gone is the magazine." He held open the heavy hotel door and gestured her inside the building. "Bermuda muggers are a strange breed."

Abby tried to check the contents of her purse as they waited for the elevator. "We could walk. It's only one flight," she offered as Blair jabbed impatiently at the button again.

"No stairs until somebody takes a look at that lump on your head," he said, appearing relieved when the doors finally opened. He motioned her ahead of him and pushed the elevator button for her floor. "Let's have your key while you're about it."

Abigail hesitated, a little bit of her old defiance surfacing at his autocratic manner. Then when she saw his worried expression and how tightly he was clenching his jaw, she relented and handed over the room key. As the elevator ground to a halt and he stepped forward to hold open the doors for her, she noted that he hadn't changed all that much despite the intervening months. Possibly his face had fined down—at a cursory glance, it seemed all angles and straight lines. The gray-eyed gaze was just as direct and penetrating—his mouth was still set in a no-nonsense mold, and there wasn't any spare flesh on the tanned skin over his cheekbones or at his stubborn chin line. The dark hair was as thick as she'd remembered, even though it was cut a little shorter so that it barely reached his collar.

Just then he wore an elegant dark sport coat that

looked as if it had come from London's Savile Row rather than Hamilton's Front Street. Transferring water from the fish pond might have dampened his cuffs but it hadn't otherwise affected his crisp gray shirt or striped tie. As his glance slid over her and his frown deepened, Abby could tell that her appearance hadn't fared as well.

Blair's concern didn't slow his steps as they went down the wide hallway to her room, and the way he pulled up in front of her door without any hesitation showed that it was familiar territory.

"Were you up here before?" she asked offhandedly as he unlocked the door and opened it wide.

He nodded, his expression darkening as the freezing temperature of the room showed the maids had set the air conditioner at "high" level. He went over to shut it off and open the glass balcony door so that the balmy outdoor air could penetrate the bedroom. "Can you get out of those wet clothes or do you need some help?" he asked, turning back to the room again.

"I can manage perfectly fine," she began and then broke off as he started rummaging in her open suitcase. "What are you doing?"

"Getting you something warmer to put on." He held up a shortie nylon nightgown with a froth of lace for a top and snorted. "That won't help. Haven't you anything sensible to wear?"

"I didn't pack for the emergency ward," she said, leaning wearily against the bedroom wall. "There are some pajamas at the bottom of the case and there's a terry robe in the closet, if that's any improvement."

He unearthed the pajamas, leaving her suitcase in a jumble, and went over to pull her robe from a hanger. His scowl came again as he noted that it, too, was only thigh-length. "This is better than nothing, I suppose," he said, and tossed the pajamas and robe in the bathroom. "Get in there and put them on while I phone hotel security and a doctor. Leave the door open."

She turned on the threshold of the bathroom, meeting his scowl with one of her own. "What for?"

"So that I don't have to call a hotel maintenance man to unlock the door if you pass out in the next few minutes."

She made an effort to keep her voice light. "I have no intention of any such thing and I don't want a doctor. At least not until I've had a chance to survey the damage. I mean it, Blair."

His eyes narrowed as her tone rose, showing that her air of nonchalance was paper thin and fraying at the edges. There was no point in upsetting things still further, he thought, and aloud said, "Okay. Just get changed. Otherwise you'll be the only person to ever die of pneumonia at this season of the year."

"All right. But I don't know what's so different about being wet now. With this humidity, I've been dripping ever since I arrived." As he smothered a grin, she remembered that earlier in the day she hadn't been reeking of fish pond, and color mounted in her pale cheeks. "Never mind—don't say anything," she told him, and went in the bathroom. She'd closed the door halfway before she recalled his warning and poked her head around the jamb to add, "I'm closing it, but not locking it. Okay?"

"Okay. I won't try any more rescue attempts unless . . ."

"I take a nose dive on the floor," she finished for him. She spared a glance at the pink tile and shuddered visibly. "I'll make every effort to avoid it."

Blair didn't hesitate before phoning the security department of the hotel, but kept an ear cocked for any suspicious silences or thuds from the bathroom. He frowned as he heard the shower turned on—wishing that he'd cautioned her against any unnecessary risks in the tub. Even though Abby hadn't been unconscious long, the bump on her head showed that she'd suffered a painful crack when she'd fallen.

When the security supervisor finally answered the telephone, Blair stated his case without being diplomatic. The man sounded shocked at the idea of an intruder on the grounds and promised that the outer premises of the hotel would be thoroughly searched. He offered the name of the hotel doctor as well as the nearest hospital, ". . . in case Miss Trent needs emergency treatment."

Blair promised to keep the hotel management advised. "Although I'd rather that she didn't have to be questioned or interviewed until tomorrow," he told the security man. "It's been an ordeal and nothing tangible can come from it." As he heard Abby open the bathroom door, he said hastily, "Right, then. She'll be in touch in the morning." He replaced the receiver and moved to turn down the twin bed nearest to the wall. "You shouldn't have washed your hair," he told her over his shoulder.

"I couldn't stand 'Essence of Fish Pond' all night. And I was careful not to touch my goose egg," she said, putting up her hand to the side of her head where her thick hair disguised but didn't quite conceal the unsightly bump. "It looks awful."

"Who cares how it looks? That's the least of your problems," he said brusquely, standing over her while she plumped the pillows so she could lean against the headboard when she got into bed. "Is there still a dry towel in the bathroom?"

She stared up at him. "I guess so. Why?"

He went into the bathroom and came out unfolding a thick pink terry. "I'm going to dry that hair." Sitting down on the side of the bed, he gingerly applied the towel to her still-damp head, taking great care to avoid the bruised area.

Abby held her breath when he first started until she saw how carefully he was going about his task. Then, when she realized she could relax on that score, she found that having his solid masculine length alongside—so close that she could feel the warmth of his thigh through the thin bed covering—was having a disturbing effect on her pulse rate.

Blair noticed her reaction almost as fast as she did. "What's the matter—is your headache worse?"

"No—it's just the same. All right, I mean."

"Any dizzy spells?"

Not that I'm going to admit, she thought, scrunching down on her pillows. It was ridiculous, she told herself, because she was the only one affected. Blair looked his usual stern self as he wielded the towel, and his stray thoughts were probably comparisons between her tousled hair and Maida's sleek, dark tresses. If that woman stumbled by a fish pond, she wouldn't end up looking like a beached whale! Abigail moaned slightly at the injustice of it all.

"What's the matter?" Blair stopped his ministrations immediately, staring at her downbent head. Gently he put a finger under her chin and looked into her face. Abby tried to hide the sudden moisture that flooded her eyes.

"I'm fine," she said crossly, brushing his hand away. "And my hair's dry enough. All I want is some sleep."

"I'm not so sure that's a good idea," he said, getting to his feet and absently folding the damp towel.

"Look, I don't mean that I can't keep awake . . ." Her words stopped when she found she was addressing his disappearing back. She sat immobile until he reappeared from the bathroom an instant later, sans towel. "As I was saying—" she began.

He cut in ruthlessly. "I heard you the first time and I don't think it's a good idea for you to be alone."

"You mean, whoever it was down there"—her hand fluttered toward the balcony—"might come back?"

Blair shook his head. "I doubt it. God knows what he was looking for, since he didn't take your purse."

"He should have made his move when I was on the way *to* dinner. Then he could have gotten Jonas' precious report to read along with the magazine."

Blair's sudden stillness was his only response, and she stared at him, trying to ignore the headache that still pounded away. Finally he moved to the other twin bed and started to turn down the spread. "That's really the reason I came to see you," he admitted slowly.

Abby bit her bottom lip to keep it from trembling. "I gathered that, but I got sidetracked by your bouquet this afternoon. What are you doing?"

"What does it look like?" He punched the pillows of the other bed into place and took off his coat and tie. "I'm the most likely baby-sitter . . ." He stopped abruptly, realizing he'd chosen the wrong word. "Most likely chaperon at this time of night," he corrected. "I'll stick around until I'm sure that you've suffered no ill effects." He sat down on the bed, winced at the firmness of the mattress, and then propped himself against the headboard. "If that report's handy, it would be a good thing to pass the time."

"You'll have to make do with a Gideon Bible. Unless you want me to retrieve Jonas' offering from the hotel's safe deposit box."

"Don't be silly!" He punched irritably at the pillows behind him and switched up the lamp on the bedside table. "You're not making any more trips outside tonight."

"Then it'll have to be the Gideon or the story of my life."

"Your uncle's kept me fairly up-to-date on that."

She raised her head to peer across at him. "Oh? Jonas didn't say anything about it." Her tone was aggrieved. "He didn't tell me what you've been doing. I didn't even know that you were still in Bermuda until he asked me to meet you here."

"*Still* in Bermuda?" he queried.

Abby leaned back, wishing that the light wasn't quite

so bright. "Your Christmas card to Jonas," she explained. "He displays them on the mantel. The note on the back didn't tell about your working at the bird refuge here, though. I didn't realize you were even connected with that kind of thing until Jonas suggested that I act as his messenger."

"I stayed on to do some research after an international conference here on sea-bird protection."

"I see." Abby's brow wrinkled as she thought about his explanation.

"Now what?"

"What do you mean?"

"Just that from your tone of voice it's obvious that you *don't* see. Or don't approve?"

"It's not any of my business," she said carefully, "except that most people have to earn a living. What happened to your law degree?"

"I got sidetracked," he said, sounding tired of the discussion as he reached over and turned off the lamp.

A faint spillover from the outside spotlights trained on the saltwater pool provided a soft glow through the room's balcony curtains, but it wasn't enough to discourage sleeping.

At least it wouldn't have been if Abigail had been in the mood for sleeping at that moment. Which she should have been, she told herself. She should have been thankful that she was safely tucked into bed with only a headache and some bruises as a reminder of her earlier ordeal.

As Blair shifted on his mattress, she reluctantly amended her thinking. The injuries weren't her real problem; Blair was. And his presence wasn't one that she could ignore or that would go away with the two aspirin she'd swallowed earlier.

It didn't help to learn that he was living a day-to-day existence on the island, cushioned by a beautiful assistant but without any serious thoughts for his future.

"There must have been a healthy inheritance," she muttered to herself.

He turned over and raised up on an elbow. "What are you talking about?"

"Nothing important," she replied, wishing she'd ignored the whole thing. "I just said you must have come into money. When you worked for Jonas, you weren't . . ."

"Quite so lucky?" He finished the sentence for her when she hesitated. "You're right. Well, this lotus-life won't last forever, but it isn't hard to take in the meantime, and the people out at the bird refuge are glad for the extra help."

"You mean, you aren't on the staff?"

"Not officially. The research has to be done, and it can't be finished without volunteers."

"Then Maida—I mean Mrs. Collins—is she a volunteer, too?"

He nodded. "Ever since her husband died a while ago. She likes to keep her hand in."

"I'll bet."

Blair's eyebrows climbed. "I'm surprised that you take that attitude. She insisted on paying you a visit."

"Complete with bouquet," Abby said flatly. There was a faint hope that Maida had merely delivered the flowers, but she knew better than to count on it.

It was just as well. Blair settled back against his pillows and confessed, "The bouquet was her idea, too. The people here are extremely friendly once they get to know you."

Especially toward a six-foot presentable male, Abigail thought, but that time had the sense to keep her mouth shut.

"You might be interested in visiting the reserve while you're here," Blair was going on. "Once you get back to feeling normal, of course. We learned that sea birds are especially vulnerable to extinction on islands like this because of man's interference. Maybe Jonas discussed the problem with you?"

"Not really." Abby was thinking that she needn't have bothered to slosh on such an ample supply of cologne after her shower. If she'd known that the main topic of bedroom conversation was going to center around some hapless ocean birds, she would have skipped the whole thing. She yawned mightily as she thought about it.

"Am I boring you?"

Blair's stiff tone made her hesitate. She wanted to tell him that if he'd offered a friendly shoulder for the discussion—instead of conducting it from the other twin bed—he could have read the room rates on the back of the door and kept her spellbound. Instead she had to say politely, "Not at all. Does it seem cold in here to you?"

That brought him upright in a hurry. "Delayed shock," he diagnosed, swinging his legs onto the floor. "Here—I'll give you the blanket from this bed."

"But you . . ."

". . . don't need it." He pulled his bed apart and, reaching across, tucked the thin blanket carefully around her. He frowned again as he surveyed the result. "You could use two or three like that."

"Maybe the housekeeper," she suggested, not thrilled with the topic, but feeling it was better than the endangered species they'd been on before. Besides, she thought with a shiver, if she didn't get warmer, she might land in that category herself.

Blair was already reaching for the phone, switching on the bed lamp at the same time to read the extension numbers on the bedside list. "I hope there's somebody on the night staff in that department," he said idly as he dialed. When the phone rang without answer, he said, "Hell!" and hung up, turning to stare bleakly down at her. "I should have taken you to the hospital."

"It would have been cheaper to just buy a blanket," she said, trying to keep her teeth from chattering.

Blair switched the light off again, but stood beside her bed, as if uncertain of his next move.

His uncharacteristic lack of assurance brought an unexpected warmth to Abby's insides and gave her the courage to say, "Perhaps we could try bundling. Just for a little while. Until I get warm."

There was an instant while he thought it over that the chill settled back down upon her, and then he said wryly, "I don't need a complete set of directions." He got one of his pillows and sat down on the edge of her bed. "Maybe if I put my arm around your shoulders . . ."

"That should help." Abby moved quickly to make space for him. "You'd better have some of the blanket."

"Don't worry about that." He slid down on the mattress, obviously trying to get comfortable after pulling her close. Abby could feel his chin against the top of her head and then his cheek as he, too, relaxed under the cocoon of bedding.

There was the faint tickle of his breath against her ear as he said, "Better?"

"Ummm."

"You don't feel like it." One of his arms tightened around her shoulders while the other rested across her waist. "This is strictly a therapeutic exercise so you can breathe once in a while and stop worrying about your virtue."

"That never crossed my mind," she flared.

"Thanks very much."

"Well, you can't have it all ways," Abby pointed out.

He started to push up on one elbow as he retorted, "I'll be damned if I . . . Oh, hell!"

"What's the matter?"

"It's not what's the matter with *me*. I keep forgetting you're the one in shock." He settled back on the pillow again, sounding resigned. "Just close your eyes, will you? This is supposed to be a rest cure—not a free-for-all."

"I'm sorry." She chewed unhappily on her lower lip and then said in an undertone, "You won't go away if I fall asleep for a while, will you?"

He made a comforting noise in his throat. "Just close your eyes. Nobody's going to play any more tricks on you tonight—or any other time. I'll do my damnedest to make sure of that."

It didn't rate with a good-night kiss or an undying pledge of affection, but at that moment, to Abigail's tired mind, it came close. She obediently relaxed against his warm masculine form and her weary eyelids drooped down. Within five minutes she was sound asleep.

Chapter Four

Blair's declaration was the first thing that came into her thoughts when she awakened the next morning. She stretched and blinked at the bright ribbons of sunlight streaming through the balcony doors, becoming aware of splashing from the swimming pool even as she shoved the covers down from her chin and sat up in bed. Sat up in solitary splendor, she discovered immediately, and noted that the pillow Blair had used was once again on the rumpled bed beyond.

She hesitated and swung her legs to the floor, wincing slightly when she attempted to smooth her hair. "Blair?" she called softly.

There was no reply from the bathroom or the balcony and then she saw the note written on hotel stationery which was propped against the mirror on the long dressing table.

"It's six-thirty and I have an early appointment this

morning," he'd written in distinctive masculine script. "I'm locking your door behind me. Take it easy today. I'll be in touch before dinner."

Abby noted the telephone number he'd provided at the bottom of the stationery with a tightening of her lips. Her gaze went to the mirror and she frowned as she saw that some buttons on her pajama coat had come adrift. Her eyes became slits of concentration as she sorted between reality and the succession of dreams she'd had during her restless night, trying to account for her strangely provocative appearance. Certainly she didn't look like a chaste bit of femininity at that moment; just the opposite. Nobody would believe that Blair had stayed overnight only in a watchdog capacity. She put such thoughts to the back of her mind and firmly buttoned the top of her pajamas, hoping that she'd looked halfway decent in her sleep.

She stared thoughtfully back to her bed, remembering that the sheet had been up by her chin when she awoke, but that didn't mean it had been that way before Blair had left.

Abby drew a deep breath and decided to be sensible. Blair was probably having breakfast at his place even then, giving thanks that his nursing stint was over.

She folded his note with a decisive gesture and was about to drop it in the wastebasket when she had second thoughts and tucked it in her purse instead. Not that she intended to call him for help—not even if her head had been falling off instead of dully throbbing at any sudden movement. She'd feel better when she had a hot shower, she told herself, and headed for the bathroom to start the prescription right away.

If Blair phoned her room to check on her progress, he'd be out of luck. She had no intention of drooping around all day, like some of those wilting flowers in her bouquet.

She did suffer some trepidation when she skirted the ornamental pool on her walk to the dining room. But even a cursory glance showed that her fear was unfounded; there was only a uniformed pool attendant on the walk by the sea wall and he was heading toward the dressing rooms with a fresh stack of pink towels. The orange cat was evidently still sleeping off his dinner somewhere, probably in the pale sunshine that had the damp concrete on the path steaming slightly—like a Wagnerian opera set for the finale. Except that it wasn't Valhalla in the background, but a busy main hotel building where the doorman and some muscular bellhops were stacking suitcases for a departing tour group.

There had been a time the night before when Abby would have given a month's salary to be leaving with them, but the combination of morning sun and palm trees brought her back to a healthier way of thinking. And Blair had nothing to do with it, she told herself, marching determinedly toward the big dining room on the mezzanine.

She was the only person going into the room, although there were several parties leaving. "You just made it, miss," a uniformed maître d' told her as she waited near his stand to be seated. "Our breakfast hours are over at ten—after that, it's room service. One good thing about coming now, you'll have a table with a view," he added, softening his attitude as he saw her guilty look at the clock.

"This is lovely," she told him as he led her to an attractive table for two by the window. "I promise to hurry."

"Enjoy your breakfast," he insisted. "We don't believe in hurrying in this part of the world." He gave her a menu, adding, "The kippers are nice this morning."

Abby was glad that he was safely out of earshot when a waiter came to fill her water glass and take her order for orange juice and an omelet. The thought of kippers —to say nothing of the smell of them—was beyond her physical state right then.

Ian came striding across a few minutes later when she was sipping her orange juice. "I thought you'd decided to give breakfast a miss," he said, looking aggrieved as he paused by her table.

Abby surveyed his tall, thin form covertly, thinking that his outfit of Bermuda shorts and sport shirt was more flattering than the trunks he'd worn by the pool the day before. "I overslept," she told him. "It's a wonder they even let me in."

"I know. I kept watching the clock while I was having my breakfast, and I've just been trying to raise you on the house phone."

"I'm sorry." She smiled apologetically. "Look, won't you sit down?"

He shook his head. "I'd like to, but the dining-room manager only let me in to give you a message."

She risked a look over her shoulder toward the

maître d'. "I see what you mean—we're both on sufferance."

"It doesn't matter. I'll have to go back to my room and get my gear to catch the next launch for the beach. If you come along, though, we can take one an hour from now."

Abigail bit her lip, trying to think of a diplomatic refusal. The prospect of sitting in the sunshine for most of the day didn't sound half as attractive just then as some quiet shade—even with Ian's likeable company as an added bonus. Besides, there was something she really wanted to accomplish first before she could feel she was on a vacation. "I'm sorry," she said finally. "Actually, I have an errand to do on St. George before I can take time off. This is partly a business trip for me, so if I want to collect a salary check next month, I'd better follow my schedule."

His eager face fell. "Damn! I'd been looking forward to buying you lunch."

"There are other days. That is, if you're going to be around for a while."

"It could depend on the weather," he said. "According to the latest reports, there's a new tropical storm south of the Bahamas that can't seem to make up its mind where it's headed."

"You mean we're actually in danger here?"

He grimaced. "Not really. These days there's plenty of warning, but the airlines and steamship companies might have to change their scheduling a bit."

"Of course. I'd forgotten you were on a layover."

"Well, I haven't." His lips curved sardonically. "So

I'm loath to give up any beach time in case I'm short-changed by the weather. How about dinner tonight?"

"You're more direct than the hurricane," she said, a smile softening her reply, "but I think I can come. Shall I phone you later this afternoon after you get back from the beach?"

He reached out to pat her shoulder. "No need. I'll call you about four-thirty if that's convenient."

"I certainly should be back from St. George by then."

"If not, I'll keep trying. Save time for a drink before dinner. And now I'd better go before I get thrown out," he said, seeing the waiter approach with her omelet. "I need to stay in good with that maître d' or we'll have a table by the kitchen door tonight."

After breakfast, Abby lingered in the lobby long enough to purchase a postcard for Jonas and then decided to mail it later at the other end of the island when she'd finished her business at St. George.

She went back to her room to get a sweater and returned the nod of a burly black maintenance man who was drinking coffee in the housekeeping room at the end of the corridor. He was still there chatting with some of the maids when she left. Abigail wanted to ask him if the marmalade cat belonged to any of the staff, and then decided against it. There was no use getting involved, especially as the cat seemed perfectly content with his life.

A half-dozen guests were sunning themselves by the pool when she went out again, and she felt a twinge of envy. If she moved a little faster, she told herself, she might get her errands done in early enough for a little tanning time, since her headache had virtually disappeared.

Her decision prompted her to take a taxi the few blocks into Hamilton's city center, but instant recall of her budget made her get out a few minutes later at the bus station by the city-hall square. Bermuda's public transportation was exceptionally good and she was soon on an uncrowded bus headed for St. George.

She felt as if she'd stumbled into a social club as the gregarious bus driver, an elderly Bermudan native, greeted most of the riders like old friends as they boarded the bus at the various stops. The latest church activities on the island were discussed at length, as well as visiting relatives. Tourists were given instructions about the proper fare and schedules in the same cheerful way. When Abby got off some forty minutes later in the center of the village of St. George, it was like leaving a friendly oasis.

Not that there was anything daunting about the colorful town where so much of Bermuda's history began. It mainly consisted of the usual tourist stores, their windows filled with Scottish woolens and British china. Tucked in at random were some small groceries where the natives shopped, and the usual tuck or sweet shops. The sidewalks were narrow and the streets curving, barely wide enough to allow two buses to pass.

Abby saw the charming facade of St. Peter's church on a rise to her left but decided to postpone visiting the oldest Anglican church in the western hemisphere until she found the art gallery which had prompted her trip.

When she'd been in Bermuda before, she'd been fortunate enough to happen on a small gallery in St. George and met the shrewd but eccentric owner, Brian St. John. He was a British expatriate whose only interest centered around the paintings on the walls of his tiny shop. Most of the works were generally uninspired local efforts destined for the lucrative and uncritical tourist market. There had been only one superb watercolor—a twisting lane bounded by stark white coral walls almost overgrown with brilliant bougainvillea and hibiscus. Abigail's lips had parted in wonder and her hushed comment of "It's magnificent" had brought an approving nod from the gallery owner.

"Naturally," St. John said, more in the manner of a curator from a renowned museum than the proprietor of a gallery which was so small that it barely deserved such a grandiose title. "The artist was Kenneth Burns. He never lacked for admirers during his lifetime, and since his death this year, even his prints are an investment."

"But this is an original, surely?" Abby had said, staring at the framed picture which dominated a wall by the staircase to the gallery's second floor.

"Of course, my dear lady. And the only one on the market in this part of the world right now." St. John had given her cotton shirtwaist an assessing glance before quoting a price for the picture well into five figures. "Very reasonable, considering the artist's reputation."

Abby winced visibly. "How much are prints of his work?"

They turned out to be expensive, too, but not completely prohibitive. There was one in stock from a numbered portfolio and Abby went home with a depleted bank balance but a Kenneth Burns print for the living room of her apartment.

It had taken months to bring her bank account into line again, but as time went by, she discovered that St. John was right—her purchase had turned out to be a good investment. Even more than that, the artist had combined his genius for color, talent for drawing, and love of the islands to bring the very spirit of Bermuda to her wall.

One good thing deserved another, she finally decided. She'd written to St. John asking if a second Burns print was available, and eventually he'd replied that he hoped to have one in the gallery in September.

Abby had made her reservations for another Bermuda vacation the next day—not wanting to spend that much money without viewing the picture in person, she told herself. Not only that—the Burns print provided a bona fide excuse in case Blair ever inquired why she'd come so far with a report that could have been sent by insured mail.

Her heart was thudding with excitement when she finally made her way to the door of the small shop. Evidently it was a day between cruise-ship arrivals, because St. George's sidewalks were blessedly without the throngs of tourists found in high season. The gallery, too, seemed deserted when she went in the door. And then a teenage Bermudan emerged from the back of the shop, putting on his moped helmet as he came.

"Excuse me," Abby said, when he started out the

front door without even acknowledging her presence. "Is Mr. St. John around?"

"Upstairs." He hesitated just long enough to jerk a thumb toward the small balcony of the gallery reached by a wide stairway. "He'll be out in a minute."

The door closed behind him and Abby saw him mount a moped which had been locked to a lamppost by the front window and take off up the street without a backward glance.

Abigail shrugged and decided to fill her time by seeing what was up for sale on the lower floor while she waited for the owner to appear. Surrealistic sunsets were evidently big, she found, grimacing with distaste as she wandered from exhibit to exhibit. There were also some far-out renditions of Bermuda landscapes with colors so violent that they could bring on a migraine if viewed for very long. Abigail completed her circuit of the room and stared impatiently up toward the loft. Maybe the delivery boy had misunderstood and Mr. St. John wasn't up there at all.

She decided to stop wasting time and go to find out. After all, there were pictures on view up there as well, so she had a legitimate excuse.

As soon as she reached the top of the stairs, she heard a voice speaking behind a closed door marked "Staff" and decided the gallery owner was simply busy for the moment. As soon as his conversation finished, she'd knock on the door and announce her presence.

More at ease by then, she wandered around the small display space in the loft, encouraged by some expensive oils, but disappointed that the Burns original she'd seen on her first visit was no longer on display.

There was another door opening off the gallery, which was partway open, and she glanced in automatically as she walked past. She stopped abruptly as she noted the very picture she was thinking about—only this time it was on the floor, propped against the wall in a small storage room. She moved closer, delighted to have another glimpse of the beautiful landscape. And then her eyes widened as she saw the collection of scattered pictures around the room; some portraits piled on a small wooden table, a few landscapes framed and stacked neatly by a cabinet, but every one showing the same dynamic style and the same rich coloring. My Lord! she thought ecstatically, an entire roomful of Kenneth Burns' paintings. She'd stumbled into a veritable treasure trove!

A brusque male voice behind her brought her abruptly back to reality. "Customers aren't allowed in here," she was told forcefully as a short man brushed past her, closing the storage-room door with a bang. "Now, then, what was it you wanted?" he went on, making no attempt to hide his irritation.

"Mr. St. John?" Abby asked, annoyed at his high-handed manner, but reluctant to stalk out of the place because of it.

"That's right. Do I know you?"

"Not unless you have an awfully good memory." Abby could have told him that she had no trouble recalling his weedy-looking chin whiskers or his thinning gray hair which matched them. He had put on a few more pounds around his waist since the last time she'd seen him, but his sharp, almost dissecting glance was the same. She remembered how it was at variance with his sloppy attire. Wrinkled cotton slacks and canvas shoes went with the haphazard displays, but he showed an astute business sense when prices were quoted.

"I'm Abigail Trent," she said, when he made no attempt to bridge the silence, merely standing in front of the closed storage room as if suspicious that she might launch herself back into it. "I wrote to you about purchasing another Kenneth Burns print."

The gallery owner's expression became more annoyed than ever as her words registered, and he nodded grudgingly. "Oh, yes, I remember something about it. We can discuss it downstairs," he added, gesturing her ahead of him. "Your letter's probably on my desk."

Abby risked another look at the closed storage room before saying, "I'm sorry about wandering off limits." As she preceded him down the rickety stairs, she added casually, "Your delivery boy gave me a wrong steer."

St. John muttered something in his chin whiskers which told what he thought of the part-time help available these days. He brushed by her and led the way to the back of the gallery, where a small desk was heaped high with letters and catalogs. Almost grudgingly, St. John pulled forward a straight chair for her, after sweeping a pile of mail onto the floor so she could sit down. "The letter must be around here somewhere," he said, pulling up a shabby swivel chair for himself and poking into the confusion on the desk.

For an instant Abby wondered if he were going to do the old W. C. Fields trick and unerringly extract her letter from the middle of the stack. She held her breath, but St. John merely stared at one or two pieces of correspondence and shoved them back atop the pile.

At that rate, she'd spend the rest of her vacation while he went on with the sifting process, Abby thought in annoyance. "It doesn't really matter," she told him. "All I want is to buy another Burns print—if it's within my price range."

"What makes you think there's any of Burns' work available?" St. John asked her, turning in his chair to face her.

It was on the tip of her tongue to say that there was plenty of evidence just upstairs, until something in his guarded expression made her think again. "Because you wrote and told me so," she said, fumbling in her purse for his letter and handing it to him.

He looked almost disappointed at such a practical response and shoved the letter back into her hands as if tired of the discussion. "There's a print of the arch out at Tucker's Town that came on the market recently. Prices have gone up, though."

"Perhaps I could see it," she began, only to have him cut her off.

"It's not here. You'll have to come back later this afternoon or tomorrow."

"Oh, but—"

"But what?" St. John interrupted aggressively.

She chewed on her bottom lip and tried to think. What was the man playing at? she wondered. Obviously he wasn't going to say a word about that fabulous collection upstairs. Under the circumstances, it seemed best to act the wide-eyed tourist.

At that moment, the sound of laughter came from the entrance of the gallery, and Abigail turned to see Blair with his hand on the doorknob, looking down at the striking figure of Maida Collins by his side. Maida's laughter stopped abruptly when she reached up to give him an impulsive hug and press a lingering kiss on his mouth.

Abby drew in her breath and turned back to St. John, but not before she caught a sideways glance from the brunette which convinced her that the embrace had been quite deliberate. Even so, Blair needn't have been such a willing victim, she thought bitterly. "I can come back later," she told St. John, who was frowning at his visitors. "I'll have to let you know when it will be."

She ignored the masculine footsteps behind her until a heavy hand on her shoulder turned her around. "What in the devil are you doing here?" Blair wanted to know. Then, belatedly remembering his manners, he lowered his voice and said, "You've met Maida."

"Of course, Blair dear," Maida Collins cut in before Abigail could reply. "You do get around, Miss Trent. Most tourists don't travel this far from the beach. I didn't know you were an art lover."

"That makes two of us," Blair said, keeping his hand on Abby's shoulder. "I thought you were going to rest all day."

Abby flashed a brilliant smile. "I can't imagine what gave you that idea."

"You *did* read my note?" he said, his grip tightening to emphasize his words.

She slid out from under with a quick movement. "Uh-huh." Then, catching a glimpse of Maida's smug expression, Abby added impulsively, "But I didn't promise anything, Blair dearest. If you'd stayed around longer this morning, I'd have made that clear."

Maida drew in her breath with a hiss, and Blair's cheeks turned dark red in the silence that followed.

Abby heard Blair mutter, "That wasn't very smart," next to her ear before he straightened, saying offhandedly, "Well, as long as you're in St. George, you might as well join us for lunch."

"What a good idea!" Maida said, seconding his suggestion with a patent lack of enthusiasm. "It can't be much fun wandering around by yourself on a holiday. Probably you would have done better to take a tour, but we can certainly show you some of the landmarks around here. My business with Mr. St. John won't take long."

"Actually, I've made other plans for the afternoon," Abby said, edging toward the door. She turned back to the gallery owner. "I'll call for an appointment tomorrow if you'll have the Burns print in by then."

Maida's eyebrows went up. "You mean you've heard of our most famous artist? Blair should have mentioned that you had such varied interests. He didn't say a word."

Abigail, hovering by the door, had an answer for that, too, but Blair shot her a warning glance as he told Maida easily, "You didn't ask." His voice sharpened then as he faced Abby. "I hope those plans of yours include some rest this afternoon. I'll be in touch about getting together for dinner."

Abigail almost informed him that she had other ideas for that time of day, too, but decided there was no point in providing more of a floor show. "We can talk about it later," was all she said before leaving the gallery.

Once outside, she didn't lose any time in making her way back to the bus stop up the street so she wouldn't run into them again. It was annoying, because she'd planned to spend the rest of the forenoon exploring the sights of St. George, which included replicas of an early dunking chair and the stocks displayed in the public square.

As she waited for a bus to come along, she saw an open red car cross an intersection a block away and recognized Maida in the driver's seat with Blair beside her. Since the car was headed toward Hamilton, Abby concluded that she needn't skulk out of St. George in such a hurry, after all. She started to stroll toward the water, remembering from her previous visit that there was a pub near the square which served sandwiches and light lunches. It was all very well to tell Blair that she had other plans for the day so that she wouldn't be an unwanted third at the table, but after turning down Ian's earlier invitation, she really had nothing more pressing than some solitary sightseeing.

She passed a winding alley and the sight of a shop owner checking his wooden window shutters inspired her to make the most of her sightseeing while she had the chance. If that tropical storm converged on Bermuda, probably the prudent thing would be to join the tourist exodus to the mainland. Considering the state of Blair's social life, she'd be smart not to stick around for more lethal blows. Maida's quick embrace at the gallery might have been calculated, but Blair certainly hadn't rejected it.

What man would? Abigail argued silently as she made her way slowly toward the town square and the pub adjoining it. Blair's brunette assistant was stunning—no doubt about it. He couldn't help but be flattered and intrigued by her interest.

Abby ordered a sandwich on the deck of the pub overlooking the harbor, and when it finally came, donated most of it to the sparrows and gulls that hovered on the railing and in the water beneath. Afterward she strolled around St. George's almost empty streets, resisting an urge to check the gallery about the availability of her Burns print.

She'd call Brian St. John from her hotel, she decided, suddenly tired of wandering around like a lost soul. The thought of lying on her room balcony in the afternoon sun was more attractive than anything St. George had to offer just then.

On the bus ride back to Hamilton, she noted a bird refuge to the right of the road and wondered if that were where Blair was spending his time. It wouldn't hurt to ask him when he phoned, she concluded. A family friend could show a normal curiosity about his work.

Her hotel room was a welcome haven after she'd walked the long blocks from Hamilton's busy center. She shivered suddenly and then shut off the air conditioner, which bathed the room with an icy chill, but did nothing to ease the humidity.

Abby took a lengthy shower, reasoning that she might as well be thoroughly wet, and after toweling off, shrugged into a full-length opaque nylon robe before reclining on her balcony lounger.

It was wonderfully peaceful there; the only sounds came from a few swimmers relaxing by the pool below and the occasional rumble of boat engines as the hotel launches headed across the waterway to the public wharf in Warwick. Abby stretched out and wriggled her toes, content to listen to the rustle of palm foliage overhead and the protesting meow of a cat.

Cat! Good Lord, what cat? Her eyes flew open and she sat up on the lounge, staring down at the lawn beyond her balcony.

There he was again! The same thin orange scavenger who'd caused her all the trouble the night before. He was picking his way through the grass, but, as if aware of her gaze, he turned at that moment and looked up at her balcony. Accusingly, as if to say, "Dinner was fine, but what's for tea?"

No way, friend, Abigail thought, hardening her resolve. A stern approach was the only way to go from now on. Then she bit her lip, wishing he had a little more to eat so those ribs wouldn't stick out quite so much.

Fortunately the telephone rang at that moment, and she went with relief to answer it.

"Abigail? Ian here. What luck to get you right off! How about our dinner date?"

Before she could reply, a light knock came from the hallway and she said, "Half a minute, Ian. There's someone at the door. I'll be right back." She put the receiver down on the bedside table and called, "Just a second," in the direction of the door but lingered long enough to check her robe, making sure that she was decently garbed for visitors.

When she opened the door, she was greeted only by an empty hallway. She frowned and stepped out to survey the corridor, but the only thing out of place was a maid's cart near the stairway. Shrugging, she closed the door again, and went back to the telephone. "Ian? Are *you* still there?" she asked, only half-joking.

"I think so. Why? Was I supposed to do a disappearing act?"

"Of course not. That only happens here, I guess. Or we've a wandering ghost on this corridor."

"You're lucky. I've a nonexistent maid on mine," he said dryly. "The bed still wasn't made when I came back from the beach. Maybe they're trying to get rid of their guests before the hurricane hits."

"Is it? I mean, is it really going to hit?" Abby asked, suddenly perturbed. It was one thing to think about a storm thousands of miles away, another to have it bearing down on the next block.

"Not for the next twenty-four hours, according to the latest. The one we've been worrying about is blowing itself out in the Atlantic. Unfortunately, it's spawned another member of the family."

"Damn!" she said softly.

"My feelings exactly. Therefore, we'd best eat, drink,

and all that folderol. We can take it step by step—starting in the bar. Say an hour from now?"

Ordinarily Abigail would have settled just for dinner, but her ego was still smarting after seeing Blair and Maida together in St. George. Why should he find her waiting meekly by the phone when he finally got around to calling?

"Abigail?" Ian asked when the silence dragged on.

"I'm still here."

"Good. I thought you might have done a disappearing act, too."

"Sorry." She tried to sound properly enthusiastic as she went on, "I'll be glad to settle for a drink and dinner—maybe here at the hotel."

He laughed. "Spoken with just the proper dash of caution. I promise not to whisk you away to any of the shadowy dens of iniquity at the far end of town. If I convince you to stay up late, there's even a hotel cabaret that's not bad."

"I saw posters of the chorus line in the lobby," she replied, unable to hide her amusement. "There was a lot of . . . talent on display."

Ian chuckled again. "I wondered if you'd noticed. Never mind, we'll take it as it comes. Meet you an hour from now in the bar off the lobby?"

"I'll be there. And thanks very much."

Her smile faded as she replaced the receiver. She knew Blair wouldn't be happy to find her among the missing, although she'd never actually agreed to a dinner date. If only he hadn't been keeping such close company with that damned brunette of his! She made a pithy comment under her breath about the state of things in general and headed for the closet to decide what to wear.

No one could have guessed the effort it took to present a lighthearted, serene appearance as she approached the hotel bar at the appointed time.

Ian, who was waiting at a small table just inside, came bounding to meet her. "How nice to see you!" he said with an approving glance that lingered on her slim black velvet suit with its silver and black iridescent taffeta jacket. "Sit down over here where I can show you off," he added, guiding her back to the table.

Abby smiled at his enthusiasm, noting that he was very presentable himself in a dark gray suit, white shirt, and regimental striped tie. After a day at the beach, his pale skin showed considerably more color than the day before. Aware of her scrutiny, he rubbed the side of his nose gingerly. "You'd think I'd know better by this time. I stayed in the sun about a half-hour too long." His gaze stayed on her face. "You look smashing!"

Which showed what the right makeup and a decent outfit could do in the way of camouflage, Abby thought with secret amusement.

"You must have had a good day—even without going to the beach," Ian said admiringly.

"It wasn't anything special. I did some shopping and then relaxed the rest of the time. I'll have to get more organized tomorrow."

"Why?" Ian gestured to a passing waiter. "You're on holiday, aren't you? What would you like?"

"Gin and tonic sounds good." She waited until he'd

ordered and the waiter had disappeared again before she asked, "Have you heard any late bulletins on the weather?"

Ian shook his head. "They parcel out the information in calculated doses. Probably don't want to send home any paying customers if there's a hope of the storm missing us."

"The natives aren't taking any chances. I saw several of the merchants down at St. George putting up shutters and taping windows today."

Ian offered cigarettes and took one himself after she shook her head. He used a match from the pack on the table and leaned back in his chair again. "That's right, you did say you were going down to that end of the island. Are you a history buff, or do you just like to tour museums?"

"Actually I was trying to pick up a watercolor." She watched the waiter put their drinks on the table and nodded her thanks as he left a saucer of salted nuts between them. "A weakness of mine," she murmured, when Ian grinned and pushed them her way.

"Good. I like to discover women's weaknesses right off. Saves a lot of time." He gave her a mock salute with his drink. "Cheers and all that."

Solemnly she touched her glass to his and echoed his toast before taking a sip.

"Now, about this picture," he said, sounding thoughtful. "Tell me more about it. I'm a bit of a collector myself."

Her eyes lit up. "Then you'll know the works of Kenneth Burns?"

"Of course. Most Bermudans do." Ian's tone was dry. "He was a famous character here for years. You must be one of those American heiresses we keep reading about, if you're in the market for a Burns painting. I understood his heirs weren't talking to anybody without a heavy checkbook."

She smiled as she shook her head. "You have it all wrong. My checkbook barely covers a numbered print. That's what I'm trying to buy—from the St. John gallery. Do you know the place?"

"I've heard of it." Ian's interest in art seemed to have faded as he reached for a handful of nuts. "So you're not an heiress after all."

"Sorry." Her lips quirked. "We could go Dutch for dinner if you'd like."

"I think I can just about manage." There was mischief in his glance as it roamed over her, lingering on the deep V neckline of her jacket. "Besides, I wouldn't mind having you a bit in my debt—if you know what I mean."

"Oh, yes," she told him dryly. "Unfortunately, you've been reading the wrong books about American women. Some of us come to the islands just to swim and have a nice quiet vacation."

"I was afraid you might see it that way." He sighed and finished his drink before setting the glass down on the table. "All right, then. Let it be understood that any overtures will be offered only in the guise of Anglo-American friendship."

Abby had trouble keeping a straight face as she asked, "You're *sure* you still want to buy my dinner?"

He laughed then and stood up, putting out a hand to pull her to her feet. "More than ever. You should know that no man can resist a challenge from a beautiful woman. Who can tell what will happen after I ply you with steak and champagne?"

From then on, his behavior couldn't be faulted. His choice of restaurant was one of the nicer parts of the hotel—an intimate hideaway whose moongate-shaped windows faced the harbor with its commuter ferries and brightly lit work boats en route to the outer islands. The restaurant itself had coral block walls and carriage lanterns to provide a flickering light in the small room. Luxuriant baskets of ferns hung from the lattice ceiling, their feathery foliage making extravagant shadows on the rough wall texture. The small hurricane lamps atop the tables provided pools of brightness to show off the white linen cloths and tasteful place settings.

"I can feel my resistance sinking by the minute," Abigail murmured, once they'd given their order and were watching a bottle of champagne being placed in a heavy silver bucket alongside the table.

Ian brightened perceptibly. "Maybe we should order another bottle chilled, just in case."

She broke into laughter and then sobered. "Seriously, I wish you'd tell me something about your work. I've never known a man before who was lucky enough to get time off in a wonderful place like this."

Her interest made Ian drop his heavy-handed attempts at flirtation and he happily regaled her with tales of his work. As a copilot for a British charter freight service, he had spent most of his time during the past year based in Bermuda. Apparently his flight plans were dictated by the cargo he carried. "Mind you, we don't have the luxury bits of the commercial flights," he told her.

"Are you talking about passengers or the stewardesses?"

He grinned and paused before taking another bite of his spinach salad. "A bit of both, actually. Of course, by now I've met most of the air crews going through here."

"So you really don't have to strike up an acquaintance at the edge of a swimming pool?" Abby queried mischievously.

He raised his glass of champagne. "That was strictly inspiration on my part. Imagine finding a lady like you unattached. Are you sure that you don't have a bloke nine feet tall to come after you at midnight and spoil things?" As he saw her sudden stillness, he lowered his glass slowly. "I knew this was too good to last. There *is* somebody lurking in the shrubbery."

"I hope not," she burst out, unnerved by his choice of words. "I mean . . . of course not. There is a man . . . but he's sort of a friend of the family—that's all."

"Bloody likely." Ian cut into his steak with such force that it shifted dangerously on the plate. "Just when we were getting along so well."

Abby winced at his vehement tone. All she needed just then was another strong-willed male in her life. "There's no need to get all upset," she soothed. "He has other interests, believe me."

"I'd like to," Ian said, still sounding skeptical.

"Take my word for it. She's a stunning brunette who lives on the island. As a matter of fact, I can't imagine how you missed her—unless she avoids hotel swimming pools."

Her soft gibe made him wince and he raised his wineglass in salute. "That's one up. Something tells me that now is the time to change the subject."

Abby put down her knife and fork on the edge of her empty plate. "All right. What did you have in mind?"

"First off, dessert." Ian nodded toward the waiter, who was wheeling a bountifully laden cart toward their table. "I can recommend the trifle—it's a specialty of the hotel."

"I couldn't, thanks. May I just settle for coffee?"

"Then you'll have to watch me indulge," Ian said, gesturing toward the trifle, resplendent in a cut-glass bowl heaped with whipped cream. The notes of a guitar coming from a musician on a tiny platform at the end of the room made Ian add, "That fellow's good. He has a real touch for the native rhythms."

Abby nodded appreciatively after listening to a complicated introduction. "He *is* good. I hope nobody minds if we drink our coffee slowly."

"This is Bermuda—remember? Nobody would mind if we spent the rest of the night here."

It wasn't that long, but it was an hour later before they started back to the lobby, amiably discussing possibilities for the rest of the evening. Ian was trying to persuade Abby that the first show of the cabaret, which started in a half-hour, would be the finishing touch.

"After all, you're on holiday," he was saying as they

approached the hotel's reception desk. "You can make up by sleeping in tomorrow morning. Mind you, if the weather cooperates, we can wander a bit on the south shore. There's a good place to eat in Somerset."

Abby looked regretfully at her watch. "I really don't think I'd better. I've sort of made other plans."

"Run up the flag! I wondered when you'd get around to them." The familiar male voice cut in so sharply that Abigail jumped a good three inches.

"Blair!" She drew in her breath, trying to cope with a pulse which had suddenly gone into overdrive. His dark suit with immaculate shirt and tie showed he'd obviously dressed for some occasion, and she swallowed, hoping that it wasn't the one that came immediately to mind. "I didn't expect to see you at this time of night."

"You could have seen me a lot earlier if you'd been around. I was just about to call the police."

She wilted visibly under his irritated look, barely remembering to say, "Ian Woodbourne . . . Blair Morley. Blair's an—"

"Old friend of the family," Ian finished for her, a rueful expression on his thin face. "She mentioned you earlier, while we were having dinner," he told Blair. "I gather there's been a bit of a mix-up."

"You could say that."

Blair didn't enlarge on his comment, and after the silence lengthened, Abby took the only way out. She turned to Ian. "I'm sorry. We'd better call it a night. Thank you for dinner. I had a marvelous time."

"We'll do it again. Soon," Ian added deliberately after

an appraising glance at the silent man standing beside them. "I'll be in touch."

Abby barely waited until Ian was out of hearing distance before she rounded on Blair. "Honestly! How rude can you get? Standing there like one of those marble pillars." She gestured toward a column by the reception desk.

"Right now I'd like to hit you over the head with one," Blair said, barely holding his temper in check. "What the devil are you playing at—standing me up after we had a date for dinner?"

"You suggested dinner," she pointed out explicitly. "We never agreed on it."

"Then you could have mentioned making other plans. Some people use the telephone."

"Only if they're told other people's home numbers. You just gave me the one at the bird refuge. I know because I checked the directory." Her chin tilted defiantly. "Why should I spend the entire day in bed?"

"In view of your latest conquest"—Blair waggled a thumb in the direction where Ian had disappeared—"I'm just as glad you didn't."

"Didn't what?"

"Spend the day in bed. Jonas wouldn't approve. Your fair-haired friend doesn't have a chin. Where did you find him?"

"There's nothing wrong with Ian's chin," she sputtered. "He's a very nice person . . ."

"Where did you pick him up?" Blair continued inexorably.

Abby was darned if she'd confess to a poolside meeting;

it was nobody's business—least of all Blair's. "When I want a chaperon, I'll let you know," she said in saccharine tones that made his jaw tighten visibly. "In the meantime, practice your Neanderthal tactics on Maida if you must. From the look of things at the gallery this noon, she apparently appreciates caveman mentality."

Her taunt failed because Blair's frown smoothed and he stared thoughtfully down at her. "You saw that display, did you? Maida's enthusiasm carries her away at times."

"How nice."

"Tuck your claws back in, girl." He paused as a sudden thought struck him. "My God, was that the reason you wouldn't join us for lunch?"

"Certainly not." Abigail kept her crossed fingers behind her slim skirt. "I had other things to do."

Blair's mouth went grim again. "So I gathered. Well, if I can interrupt your busy schedule, maybe you'd get that report of Jonas' out of the safe-deposit box for me. Unless you have other plans for the rest of the night."

"You're a fine one to talk about claws. If I didn't know better, I'd think you were jealous."

"You always were a great one for adding two and two to come up with five. Just get the report like a good girl and then I'll walk you back to your room."

"You don't have to treat me as if I were ten years old," she said, drawing herself up to her full height.

Blair's glance roamed over her stiff figure, but she could tell that he wasn't admiring her measurements or the outfit which had earned Ian's compliments earlier.

"Get the report, Abigail," Blair told her when his gaze encountered hers once again. "It's late."

She whirled and made her way to the cashier's cage to sign the safe-deposit card. The way things were going, she couldn't wait to put Jonas' report in Blair's hands. After that, there was no reason that she'd have to see him again before she left the island.

Blair was propped against the marble pillar they'd mentioned earlier when she emerged with the report in its manila envelope. "I want to look it over, but not here," he said, taking it from her and giving a cursory glance around the lobby, which had suddenly become crowded with an arriving tour group. "We'll go back to your room."

Abigail opened her lips to protest, but the brighter light by the reception desk showed the drawn look on his face which she hadn't noticed in their earlier fracas. He couldn't have had much sleep the night before, she thought guiltily. Probably her tossing about and nightmares in the aftermath of shock had contributed to his short temper. That—and being stood up, as well. She closed her mouth and swallowed. "All right. Did you ever have anything to eat?"

"I'll make a sandwich when I get back to my place," he said, tucking the report under his arm and steering her toward the lobby entrance. "It doesn't matter—I had a big lunch."

And a long one, I'll bet, Abigail thought. The very idea of it made her remove her elbow from his grasp once they got outside the main building and started down the path toward her wing.

The quiet darkness settled like a cloak around them as they followed the scattered lights which marked the edge of the pathway, making for the lighted entrance ahead of them. When they neared the reflecting pool, Abby shot a nervous glance toward the shaded area at the bottom of the big palm tree, but it seemed just as deserted as the rest of the hotel grounds.

"I don't know where everybody goes," she said, managing not to look over her shoulder as they passed a towering hedge which cast them in even a deeper shadow. "The lobby of this place resembles Penn Station, but the minute you go out the door—it's like being thrown away. Not even a cat tonight. Although he was around this afternoon."

"Maybe he wanted to eat early and when you didn't show up tonight, he made the rounds of the neighborhood." Blair slowed to give her a suspicious look as they came into the light again. "Have you any more rations for him hidden in your purse?"

"Not tonight."

"What's the matter? Afraid to shock your friend by asking for a doggie bag after dinner?"

"Not at all. We had steak, so it wasn't worth the effort. Cats are apt to be finicky. Besides . . ." Abby rounded on him fiercely as they reached the door. "Whose team are you on? Last night you thought I needed certifying because I was handing out leftovers on the lawn. Now it's a different story."

"Okay"—he gestured her ahead of him as he held open the door—"I get the point. Do we take the stairs tonight or wait for the elevator?"

"Don't change the subject."

"In that case, we'll take the stairs," he said, steering her that way. "If you're out of breath, I'll get off easier."

"An apology might be more effective," she said, starting up the carpeted steps to the second floor.

Blair's shoulders shook with laughter. "If that isn't like a woman! I'm the one who was stood up for dinner, but I'm still expected to come through with an apology."

Abby was glad to have an excuse for her silence as they finished the second flight and she leaned against the banister at the top, still breathing hard. "I'm out of condition," she explained.

"If you'd gotten some rest today," he began, and then paused, his expression resigned. "What do you say to a truce? I'm too damned tired to keep on fighting."

"I'm glad," she said simply. "So am I. And I *am* sorry about spoiling your evening. Especially after you were so nice to me last night."

"There's still some time left," Blair said, walking beside her down the quiet hotel corridor. "I see what you mean about this place being deserted. You'd think there'd be some staff in evidence."

"I heard a woman complaining at breakfast about waiting two hours for extra towels." Abby fitted her key into the lock on her door. "I almost suggested that she try the swimming pool. They had stacks of them there yesterday. Oh, Lord! Now what?"

The last came as an agonized wail when she crossed the threshold to find the contents of her suitcases thrown haphazardly on the floor.

"Damn it to hell!" Blair said, pushing her aside to

check the empty bathroom and the long closet beside the door.

"What is it about this place?" Abby asked, sinking unhappily onto the side of the closest bed and surveying her ransacked belongings. "It's supposed to be one of the nicest hotels in Bermuda. I feel as if I'm in the middle of a crime wave. Maybe it would be simpler if I just went home."

"I think it would." Blair went back to close the hall door and slide the chain lock on as an added precaution. "You shouldn't put all the blame on the hotel, though. I should have warned you when you arrived, but Jonas and I didn't think you'd get involved." Her wide-eyed stare made him grimace apologetically, and he sat down on a straight chair facing her as he said, "There's a bit more to my work here than bird-watching."

Abby's eyebrows drew together in sudden suspicion as his meaning dawned. "Or maybe it's a different kind of bird."

He nodded slowly. "A lousy species—involved in more kinds of contraband than you'd believe. Currently, they're using Bermuda as a transfer spot on the money trail."

"You'll have to explain that, you've left me behind."

"I'm sure you've heard about the illegal profits that Florida authorities are encountering in connection with drug trafficking from South America?" When she nodded, he went on. "That's just the first step in a thing called money laundering. The next step comes when the racketeers turn that money over to companies operating as fronts for them. After that, the cash is transferred to foreign countries under the guise of regular investments. That's where Bermuda comes in these days. They're using the island as a cache and transfer point. The Florida authorities are tightening the noose there, and Bermuda makes a good alternative. It's a handy location geographically—just hours from Europe for investments or a short hop to South America to check supply sources."

"But you must have some leads on who's doing it."

"Naturally." He sounded almost impatient. "But that's a hell of a long way from conclusive evidence, and I'm talking about people who are dealing with heavy money. Right now, I'm sorry that I ever let Jonas talk me into this investigation—even as a temporary assignment."

"So you're smack in the middle of it!"

He nodded. "And until yesterday, I thought I was doing a pretty good camouflage act. Damned if I know what got our friends here excited. Probably your family connection with Jonas."

"So he didn't sever all his ties with federal drug enforcement when he retired," Abby said, sounding exasperated. "I'm really not surprised. He can't resist getting involved."

"These days, experienced help is hard to find."

"And you! I thought you just needed a job when you worked with him at the clinic."

"I did. Later, the background came in handy for this. There was no need to trump up fake credentials when I arrived." His stern mouth softened. "I'm doing some valid research on their endangered seabirds."

"Only you didn't know that I was going to be one of them."

The amusement abruptly left his face. "You're right about that. Until that attack last night, and now this . . ." He gestured at the shambles around them. "Well, there's only one thing to do—move you out of here. Do you need my help getting your belongings together? If not, I'll look over this report while you're doing it."

"Hold on a minute!" She bounced to her feet as he reached for the manila envelope she'd retrieved from the safe-deposit box. "What do you mean? Move me out? Where in the dickens do you think I'm going?"

"My place, of course. You can live with me for a while." He stared somberly across at her. "At this point, I'd a hell of a lot rather have you play the role of a fallen woman than a dead one."

Chapter Five

"Is it a multiple-choice question?" Abby asked after a long moment of silence.

"What are you talking about?"

"Well, I'm not keen on your solution, so how about 'none of the above'?" Then she put up her palms to her hot cheeks as the enormity of the situation registered. "I feel as if I'd been shoved into the last reel of a horror show without a script. Are you serious about all this?"

He jerked a thumb at her vandalized possessions. "What does it take to convince you? Whoever did this has the wrong game plan, but how in the deuce do we get that message across? Of course, you could always go back home," he added hopefully.

Since that was an alternative that she'd considered earlier, Abby should have agreed without hesitation, suggesting that he call the airport for a seat on the first plane out. It was absurd to hear herself protesting,

"What about my vacation? Besides, with the storm warning, Ian said all flights would be fully booked."

"Ah, yes—Ian." Blair ground out the words with heavy irony. "Did he have any other suggestions?"

"Nothing that could possibly concern you." Abby set about righting her largest suitcase on the end of the bed. "Is your place nearby?"

Blair's mouth slanted in a reluctant grin. "I gather you've made up your mind?"

"Well, it was a limited choice." She bundled up some lingerie and stuffed it in the top of her bag as she noticed his interested gaze. "What excuse do I give for leaving early?"

"I'm not sure that checking out officially would be a good idea. How about taking just enough for overnight, and we'll see how things go in the morning. There's nothing missing, is there?"

She ran her eye over her belongings quickly before shaking her head. "Actually, there isn't anything of value. The only jewelry is costume—except for what I'm wearing—and I had my extra traveler's checks in the safe-deposit box."

"Along with this report," he said, looking down at it thoughtfully.

She frowned as she followed his glance. "Is that about birds? Real birds, I mean."

He laughed and started to leaf through Jonas' offering. "For the most part, I'm sure it is. But I did mention at the refuge that I hoped to receive some new waterfowl statistics in the next few days. Our friends must have let their imagination do the rest."

"Did you ever mention my connection with Jonas?"

"Only in passing. He's an acknowledged expert on wild birds, so there didn't seem to be any danger. And, as far as you were concerned . . ."

When he broke off, shrugging, her eyebrows came together in suspicion. "Go on. What about me?"

"Well, sex is one thing that all parties understand."

Abby's mouth dropped open. "You did say 'sex'?" she got out finally.

"Don't look so amazed," Blair countered irritably. "I had to have some explanation for your appearance. I let it slip out that we had a relationship a couple of years ago. There was no need to go into details."

"I see. So I don't have to worry about my reputation if I move in with you. It's already taken a dive."

"Dive?"

"Fallen woman," she explained tersely. "I suppose I've been pining away in the interim and come here begging for you to take me back?"

Blair made a point of thumbing through the report, keeping his glance on the printed pages as he mumbled, "Something like that."

"Oh, great."

"Well, I had to think of some excuse. Are you going to pack that stuff?" he asked, taking the offensive.

"Maybe you'd like to tell me how to do that, too."

"There's no need to get your dander up. Jonas would have my head if anything happened, so we'll take extra precautions. Besides, what's the difference whether you sleep at my place or I stay here? It's just more convenient this way, and frankly, that mattress"—he jerked his chin toward the second twin bed—"leaves a lot to be desired."

His comments effectively put the damper on any other objections she might have mentioned. The reference to Jonas had made her feel like a piece of unwanted luggage, and she didn't think men who'd spent the night with a woman usually complained about the quality of the mattress. The hell with it, she thought disconsolately. Tomorrow she'd see about getting reservations home.

She pushed a pair of silk pajamas into her smaller suitcase and closed it before putting it at the end of the bed. "I think that's everything," she said, walking over to the closet and extracting her nylon raincoat. "It's a good thing it's dark. Otherwise the hotel would think I was skipping out without paying." She lingered to consider the two beds, with their unwrinkled bed linen.

Blair nodded at her questioning gaze and picked up the suitcase. "I agree. Rumple one up. No use starting any more rumors than necessary."

"Right." Abby walked over to her bed and jerked the sheet and spread into disarray, finishing by trying to make a dent in the pillow.

"Good luck," Blair said sardonically as she pounded without success. "I tried to do the same thing with my head all night and didn't succeed then either. Too bad that the people who buy hotel furnishings don't have to sleep on them. Ready?"

"I guess so." She started toward the door, pausing just long enough to frown down at her watch. "What time is it?"

Blair consulted his own and told her. "What's the matter," he asked her. "Doesn't yours work?"

"Sort of." She pulled the nylon raincoat over her shoulders and checked her purse to make sure that she had the room key.

"That's a silly remark," Blair persisted. "Watches either work or they don't."

Her lips tightened. "If you must know, it hasn't lost more than three seconds since I bought it two weeks ago. I thought a digital one that you didn't have to wind would be good for traveling."

"Well, then . . ."

"Unfortunately, the jeweler set it to tell time in San Francisco or Seattle or Los Angeles. Not Bermuda. It's five hours off and I'm tired of trying to remember."

"That's easy. Just reset it."

"There's nothing worse than a man who states the obvious," she snapped, waiting for him to open the hall door. "I would have reset it if I knew how. I left the instruction book at home. Once I got here, I didn't have the nerve to go into a jeweler's and ask them to set my watch for me. It's like asking somebody to"—she waved a distrait hand—"to . . . to cut your meat. I'd have felt like a perfect fool. Stop laughing, you idiot. I'm sorry I mentioned it."

Blair was still chuckling as he pulled open the door. "Never mind. I'll try to figure it out tonight when we get to my place. At least you didn't give up and buy another watch set to Bermuda time." He caught sight of her suddenly heightened color. "My God, you didn't!"

"I just thought about it," she admitted. She watched

him close the room door and survey the deserted corridor before he led the way toward the elevator. "What about your report? Wouldn't it be better off in the safe-deposit box?"

"There's nothing in it that couldn't be published on the front page of the paper except that there'd be an awful drop in circulation. Statistics on the decrease in endemic birds have the same reader appeal as the mating habits of the tsetse fly."

"But you still think it triggered all the trouble?"

"The tsetse fly?"

"Be serious, will you?"

Blair sighed as he pushed the elevator button. "Darned if I know. None of it makes any sense—except that Jonas should never have let you get on the plane."

She thought about that until they were in the elevator and on their way to ground level. "Of course, there's another way of looking at it."

"What's that?"

"Well, if they'd really wanted to hurt me, they had plenty of chances. Like today—I was all over the island."

"I know," Blair said in some resignation. He held open the elevator door as they reached the ground floor, giving a satisfied nod when he saw the deserted entranceway and foyer. There was a sound of voices from a service room part way along the lower hall, where a maid's cart still stood, but apparently the night staff was staying out of sight. "Now I understand why this hotel is so popular with honeymooners," Blair said as he walked toward the entrance. "There isn't one chance in a million that you'd be disturbed."

Abby stayed close by his side as they started toward the main building once again. "I'm not sure that I like being so exclusive."

"My feelings exactly. At least where I live, the walls are so thin that I can give you the life story of the people who have the apartment upstairs." He caught her elbow as they came to an intersection in the path and steered her toward the hotel's parking area, pulling up beside a compact car by the curb. "This belongs to me, so we can skip walking along the deserted street."

"No romance in your soul," Abby said in mock reproof.

She slid into the front seat of the small car after he'd tossed her suitcase in back, and waited for him to come around to get behind the wheel. "I think the only action must be in the cabaret," she added as he pulled out onto a quiet thoroughfare and turned right along the waterfront.

"Las Vegas and Atlantic City don't have to worry. There *is* one place still open," he informed her, making a left turn when they reached a small business area, finally pulling up in front of a lighted grocery. "I'd better get some food, since you'll be staying for breakfast." He turned off the ignition and turned to face her. "Back in a minute. Okay?"

She nodded and watched him disappear into the store. It was more like five minutes before he returned with a bag of groceries, which he promptly put in her lap.

"Hang on to it—there are eggs and milk," he said briefly.

"Okay. I promise not to squeeze." She was peering into the top of the paper bag while they were still in the lighted forecourt of the store. "Filled milk?" she said incredulously, reading the words on top of the carton. "Filled with what?"

Blair chuckled as he pulled back out onto the street. "Just the usual vitamins. Actually, it's Bermuda jargon for reconstituted. There's fresh milk available in the groceries most of the time, but at this hour . . ." He shook his head. "The filled stuff isn't bad."

"It'll be fine," she said hastily. "I forgot about being in the middle of the Atlantic. The food here has been great."

"You'd be doing my stomach a favor by changing the subject. It's used to three meals a day, and right now I can distinctly feel my backbone."

Abby cast a guilty look at his profile. "We can fix something when we get to your place," she said, hoping to make up for his lost dinner.

"It's too late to bother." He slowed and pulled into a brick courtyard in front of a Mediterranean-style building which, like Abby's hotel, apparently faced the harborside.

From what she could see, that was all the two buildings had in common. The structure in front of her was only three stories and seemed to ramble in haphazard fashion, as if the owners had added new parts whenever the urge took them. There was the usual lush shrubbery hanging over a moongate doorway, and Abby took time to appreciate the charm of the courtyard before she got out of the car. "This place looks nice," she said, keeping a firm grip on the groceries as she buttoned her raincoat. "It's not very big, is it?"

"About ten or twelve flats, I guess. I was lucky to get a sublet. Maida told me about the place."

He could have talked all night and not mentioned that bit of information, Abby thought, as her spirits took a dip.

"How nice." She moved quickly through the entranceway as he held the door. Ahead of her there was a small lobby stuffed with chintz-covered furniture—where worn red velvet drapes almost covered the windows along one side. A stone fireplace took up a good part of another wall, but it was almost impossible to see the logs stacked in the firebox because of an intricate brass screen and a set of fire tongs big enough to handle small trees. Just beyond the fireplace a parrot stared stolidly out at them from a wrought-iron cage. As Abby stood there, an elderly woman poked her head around another doorway, but hastily departed, trailing a chiffon scarf like a disappearing wraith.

Abby's lips quivered in sudden amusement and she turned back to Blare. "The decor's straight out of the twenties. Do they serve martinis in coffee cups?"

He surveyed the lobby thoughtfully. "You might be right. I've often wondered how they kept the dining room solvent—the food's terrible."

"But I thought this was an apartment house."

"Not entirely." He nudged her toward the stairway to their right. "There are a few hotel rooms. Mainly to keep the residents happy when their friends arrive in town."

"Well, why couldn't I—?"

"No deal," Blair cut in, not bothering to let her

finish. "The place is jammed to the rafters right now. Here we are." The last came when he pulled up at a door close to the head of the stairs.

Abby noticed that the management didn't waste any electricity in lighting the corridor either, but, unlike her hotel, she could hear music wafting down the hallway and voices from below as the front door opened again.

"See what I mean," Blair commented as he led the way into his apartment. "There's no chance of anything going undiscovered around here. And I mean *anything*. By now, they've probably already set a place for you in the dining room. Anybody who tried to sneak in would be collared for a fourth at bridge before he could reach the second floor," he added somewhat bitterly.

He crossed the living room to open another door, which revealed a bedroom, made even smaller-looking by the dark red plush spread on the double bed and an overpowering pair of draperies made of the same fabric which covered the window. "There's a saving grace," Blair told her as he put her suitcase down on a low chest. "In the daytime, the harbor view makes up for any deficiencies. Like lukewarm water . . ." The last came as he showed her the old-fashioned bathroom opening off the bedroom, where a claw-footed tub and pedestal washbowl were immaculate but showed signs of the years.

"You'd never make a real-estate salesman," Abby said as she peered around his shoulder and watched him close the door. She pointed toward a mahogany fixture at the other side of the living room. "What's behind the screen?"

"In the brochure, it's called housekeeping facilities," Blair said, going over to push it aside, revealing an electric plate on a Formica counter, a small sink, and an apartment-sized refrigerator tucked in the corner. He took the bag of groceries that Abby was still clutching and stowed away the milk and eggs in the refrigerator before putting cold cereal and a few other basics in a cupboard above the stove. "The management prefers that we eat in the dining room, so they don't encourage do-it-yourself efforts. This is more convenient for breakfast unless you prefer tea and cold toast downstairs."

"I'm sure it will be fine," Abby said demurely.

His eyebrows went up. "That sounds like a direct quote from the etiquette book. Is Bermuda getting to you, or have you suddenly decided that I don't come with a set of horns as standard equipment?"

"Who knows?" Abby tried to keep her tone as flip as her words. Her air of disdain and hauteur was hard to maintain in view of his recent actions. It was also hard to ignore his masculine appeal in the crowded apartment, where everything smacked of his occupation: a stack of ornithology books on a piecrust table at the end of the davenport, a pair of golf shoes protruding from under an upholstered chair, and a nylon rain jacket hanging from the knob of the closet door. Blair took it and stuffed it inside, saying, "I'm sorry about the mess. I didn't plan on having company. You can put your coat in here or use the closet in the bedroom. I'll get my stuff out of there right away."

"What for?"

Abby's blunt query caught him unawares. She could

tell that by his suddenly arrested movement in the midst of closing the closet door. He turned slowly. "What did you say?"

"I just meant that you didn't have to move out of the other room," she said hastily, suddenly aware that her words could have been taken another way. "There's no reason why you should have to leave your bed." As he continued to frown at her, she realized that she still hadn't spelled it out. "I can sleep here on the couch," she said, trying to ignore the sudden warmth in her cheeks. "It's more my size than yours, and besides . . . I won't hear of it any other way."

"Giving ultimatums now, Abby?"

His soft challenge made her flush even more. "I didn't mean it like that. Please, Blair, be sensible. There's no need to inconvenience you any more than necessary."

"There is another alternative," he pointed out after a moment's pause, but then, without giving her a chance to reply, went on levelly, "Unfortunately, Jonas wouldn't approve. I'm not so sure that it's a good idea myself."

Damn the man! thought Abby angrily, her lips tightening. Just as if she didn't have anything to say about the matter. Not that she'd have gone along—even on a platonic basis. Which, of course, it would have been. "It's nice we all agree," she pointed out, not bothering to hide her sarcasm. "I prefer the couch, thanks."

"I wonder if you would." Blair's words were hardly audible as he leaned negligently against the wall. He straightened and then shrugged, obviously fed up with the senseless discussion. "I'll get the sheets and blanket. If you want anything to eat, now's the time."

Abby watched him disappear in the bedroom, closing the door behind him, and slowly went over to pour herself a glass of milk—more for something to do than anything else. Afterward, she rinsed out the glass and put it in the cupboard before sitting on the edge of the couch.

The bedroom door opened abruptly behind her and Blair came back in the room, this time wearing pajamas and robe and carrying a stack of clean linen plus a pillow. Abigail bounced to her feet as he approached.

"I put a clean towel on the hamper," he said as he started assembling the makeshift bed. "If there's anything else you need, let me know."

"I can help you with that," Abby said, trying to get close enough to smooth the sheets on the lumpy couch cushions.

"No need. I don't like them tucked in," Blair said, reaching for a blanket.

"But I said that *I'd* sleep here," she protested.

He did nothing to hide his irritation as he towered over her. "Look! There's a time to give up, and this is it. You're not winning, and if you keep on arguing, you might get more than you bargained for. My polite inclinations run thin at this time of night, so you'd better stop while you're ahead."

There was something lurking beneath the surface in his voice that made Abigail swallow and decide not to risk further debate. It was one thing to share the cage of the tiger; only a fool risked tweaking his nose.

She nodded and started toward the bedroom.

"One more thing . . ."

Blair's rough command stopped her in her tracks. "Tomorrow, don't head for any lonely beaches or solitary walks," he said. "As a matter of fact, if the weather report stays threatening, you'd better finish up any last-minute errands."

"You make it sound as if doomsday is approaching," she said, trying to keep her voice uncaring.

"You've got it all wrong again. The way things are, a hurricane gives you the ideal reason to leave. No one would give it a second thought."

Her chin went up. "Except me. I didn't come all this way just to turn around and go back. Why, I haven't even got my Kenneth Burns print yet, and there's some perfume that I promised a friend of mine."

"Kenneth Burns, the watercolorist?" Blair asked, ignoring her last objection.

"That's right. He's the reason I was at the gallery today. Mr. St. John is trying to find a Burns print for me."

Blair flipped the pillow he was holding onto the end of the couch and went over to turn off the overhead fixture, leaving the room with only the dim light of a floor lamp, topped by a Tiffany-type shade. "I thought Burns died recently," he said.

"He did. That's why it's so hard to find anything of his on the market now."

For an instant, Abby was tempted to mention the display of Burns' works that she'd seen in the storage room of the gallery and then she noticed how Blair was rubbing the back of his neck as he walked across to the small refrigerator. If she'd ever seen a man who didn't want to have an extended discussion on Bermudan art, Blair was a prime example.

"Anyhow," she said stiffly, "I don't want to leave here without one if I can help it."

He extracted the quart of milk and poured some in a glass. "Want to join me?"

"No, thanks. I had some."

He nodded and turned to face her, glass in hand. "Then tomorrow I suggest you finish your business at St. George. There's another cruise ship due in, so you're not apt to be caught wandering alone. I'm sorry that I can't take time off now to shepherd you around."

Like an unwanted maiden aunt, Abby thought dispiritedly, and that's the way he was looking at her just then. A careful, measured appraisal that was a far cry from the expression he'd shown earlier. It simply wasn't her night, she decided as she opened the bedroom door. "I'll manage, thanks."

"I never doubted it," he mocked. "I'll leave a duplicate key to the apartment on the table if I don't see you in the morning."

"That won't be necessary. After all, I have a perfectly good hotel room of my own."

"And you'll give it a wide berth unless I'm with you," he ordered calmly.

"But that's ridiculous," she sputtered.

"Maybe. But we'll play it my way all the same. And just so we don't have any more mix-ups, tomorrow night we're having dinner together." He swallowed the last of his milk and rinsed out the glass with an economy of motion. "That means you and me. No Ian. You understand?"

"There must be something about the weather here that goes to your head—what size in hats do you wear these days?"

He walked across the room and pulled up deliberately in front of her, tightening the belt on his robe. Almost as if he had to find something to occupy his hands when his expression showed that he was tempted to put them tightly around her throat. "I asked you a question," he said levelly, "and I'd like the courtesy of an answer. Especially since the object is to have you leave Bermuda in the same condition that you arrived."

"Did it ever occur to you that I'm responsible for that? And also my friends. What's wrong with Ian?"

"Not a damned thing that I know about."

"That's what I mean. I'm not tossing around orders about your friends. Like Maida . . ." Her voice trailed off expectantly, hoping he might explain just what kind of a relationship he had with the beautiful British woman.

"Maida's my business," he said in a tone that brooked no interference and showed any discussion on that subject was closed. "Now, are we settled on dinner?"

"Oh, all right." It was scarcely a gracious reply, because Abby was ready to weep with frustration by then. "If there isn't anything else," she said through clenched teeth, "do you mind if I go to bed?"

"That *was* the idea I was trying to get across."

"Well, you've succeeded—so go to the head of the class," she flared, and turned to sweep into the bedroom. In the process of slamming the door behind her, the knob caught on the pocket of her slim velvet skirt, making her stumble awkwardly back toward Blair, who instinctively caught her in his arms before she fell.

It was hard to tell exactly what happened next. Abby only knew that somehow Blair's grip had shifted and, an instant later, his mouth came down on her parted lips with devastating possession. She was vaguely conscious of twining her own arms around his neck as the kiss hardened and Blair molded her against his lean body. If there hadn't been so many skyrockets going off in her mind, Abby could have concentrated on the havoc that his hands were causing as they moved down from her shoulders to settle purposefully on her hips. She *did* know that she finally had to breathe, and it was with reluctance that she pushed back from his clasp to accomplish it.

Blair seemed to be having trouble with his own breathing just then as he stared down at her, his glance dark and brooding. His eyes moved toward the double bed in the room beyond and Abby inhaled sharply, wondering what his next words would be.

When they finally came, she didn't know whether to laugh or cry. His voice had a rough undertone, but that was the only evidence of emotion. "I didn't plan on that happening, and I don't intend to apologize," he said tersely. "I suggest you forget it because it's better that way. Now—go to bed." He put his palm in the middle of her back and shoved her—there wasn't any other word for it—into the bedroom so he could close the door firmly between them.

Chapter Six

After that kind of leave-taking, Abigail had every reason to hope that the next day would be better. The odds were certainly in favor of it, considering all that had happened to her since her arrival. Unfortunately, as soon as she saw the note propped against her bed table on awakening, her spirits sank. "Don't forget!" Blair had underlined the words in very black ink: "Don't go off by yourself and don't be late for dinner!"

As a *billet-doux*, it ranked even below a "payment-due" reminder from Internal Revenue, Abby thought as she got out of bed.

There were other things which seemed to fall into the same dismal category—the sun had disappeared and raindrops were haphazardly attacking the window when she pulled back the drapes to stare out onto the harbor. At least Blair wouldn't have to worry about her lolling on the beaches. She'd reflected on that while she made toast and coffee for breakfast and ate standing up, staring out the window onto the choppy waves which hurled themselves against the apartment breakwater. Even so, she wasn't going to spend the day in seclusion just because of a little rain. She owned a raincoat, and besides, there was a smidgen of blue sky to the west. There was also an inordinate amount of wind, she discovered as the trees lining the edge of the property bent suddenly under a severe gust. It could mean that the newest storm was heading north and east after all. If that were the case, she didn't have any time to waste.

She changed into a ginger-colored corduroy skirt topped by a plaid blouse of similar tones which boasted a white pique collar and cuffs. The outfit wouldn't suffer from a little rain, and her all-weather coat looked fine as a topper.

A few minutes later she discovered that Blair had a private phone which made it easy to call the St. John gallery and check on her Burns print. A singsong native voice answered, saying that Mr. St. John wasn't in at the moment and he hadn't left any messages for Miss Trent. Not only that, the man at the other end of the wire didn't know anything about a Burns print and suggested languidly that she call later.

"When will Mr. St. John be back?" Abigail asked hastily, before she could be cut off.

"I have no idea, miss."

"Well, could I leave my number?"

"It would be better if you called this afternoon. He should be in after lunch."

"And when's lunch?"

"Between twelve and two—as is customary." The man's tone showed what he thought of that question.

"All right—but will you please tell him I called?"

"If you wish, miss."

Abigail hung up with more force than necessary, suspecting that her last request would be buried or ignored. Well, if worst came to worst, she could conclude the transaction by mail, she told herself, and reached for the telephone directory again.

She was interrupted by a token knock from the hallway and glanced up, startled, when a uniformed maid unlocked the door.

The portly, middle-aged black woman looked equally surprised and peered over her shoulder at the number on the door—as if assuring herself that she was in the right place. "Mistah Morley?" she asked, her eyebrows drawing together suspiciously.

"He's gone to work," Abby said as casually as she knew how. So much for the apartment's vaunted grapevine, she thought, hoping that her flushed cheeks didn't confirm her guilty feelings. Damn Blair! Why hadn't he said there was maid service? At least the sheets and blankets still folded on the end of the couch helped her alibi. "Mr. Morley's an old friend of mine," she told the woman, who was still hovering on the threshold, clutching her vacuum cleaner. The words were no sooner out than Abby saw *that* explanation wouldn't help her cause or her reputation. Taking the offensive might be best. "I won't be in for lunch and I'm not sure about dinner. Would you pass the information along, please," she told the woman, getting to her feet and reaching for her coat, which she'd left over a chair. "Terrible weather, isn't it?" she tossed over her shoulder as she stepped around the rest of the cleaning paraphernalia and made her escape.

Fortunately, the lobby was deserted, as was the small reception desk in the corner. Abby stopped long enough to shrug into her topcoat and put a scarf over her head, managing to get out the front door just as an older woman who had "manageress" written all over her stern visage emerged from the dining-room archway.

It was all very well for Blair to talk about new freedoms and casual rules of behavior, Abby decided as she walked to the street, her head bent against the light rain. Except that he didn't stick around to make any of the explanations. It was doubly annoying to feel guilty, since nothing had happened, she reflected, and startled a passerby on the sidewalk with a fervent "Dammit!" as she thought about it.

Despite the weather, there were plenty of people in the streets, including the usual quota of moped riders, who were mostly encased against the rain. They presented an incongruous appearance; the women in their high heels and silk dresses under plastic coats and businesslike safety helmets. The men combined abbreviated rain jackets with Bermuda shorts; apparently damp, bare knees didn't bother them at all!

Abigail grimaced as rain trickled down her collar, and set off purposefully toward her own hotel, determined to buy a small umbrella after she checked to see if there were any messages at the desk.

There weren't, which showed Ian had apparently

given her up as a poor prospect. It was just as well, she thought honestly. Then she ducked into a gift shop off the lobby and purchased a collapsible umbrella to make the rest of her wanderings more comfortable.

By then, it was close to lunchtime, and she hovered on the hotel's front step, wondering whether to walk into the main business section of Hamilton or be extravagant and take a taxi.

An elderly driver seemed to sense her indecision and pulled up from his place in the taxi rank to say, "Like a ride to town, miss? This rain isn't going to go away."

Abby nodded, glad that he'd made up her mind for her. "I know," she said, getting in the back of the small car with relief. "Except that it isn't a long walk and I really need the exercise. Could you take me to the middle of the shopping district on Front Street, please?"

As the man drove, he proved a fund of information about the hours of the perfume factory she wanted to visit later in Somerset by the Maritime Museum—even to the extent of advising her which bus to take from the square.

After they parted, Abby wished that she'd asked him if he could have driven her for part of the afternoon. Then she remembered the local taxi rates for charter, which were posted everywhere, and shook her head. If she wanted to have any money left for shopping, she'd better stick to public transportation.

The decision made her feel so virtuous that she had a splendid lunch in the coffee shop of one of the fine specialty stores and later splurged on a cashmere cardigan which was too good a bargain to ignore.

Afterward, she window-shopped at some of the Hamilton art galleries on her way to catch a bus and tried phoning Brian St. John again, only to have the phone ring unanswered.

At least that helped her to make up her mind that the perfume factory at the other end of the island was her next order of business, and she waited in line at the downtown coach terminal.

There was almost a full coach of shoppers, who sat steaming in their damp coats and soggy shoes as the woman driver started toward the south shore of the island. The rain outside settled to a steady drizzle. Not that it mattered, Abby reassured herself stoutly. If she had her directions right, the bus should go fairly close to the perfume factory, located at the end of the island archipelago close by the Maritime Museum and Keepyard. Once she completed her business, she'd take the local ferry back to Hamilton.

She deposited her umbrella on the floor by her feet and settled back. The woman who was seated next to the window was forty pounds overweight and carried a lumpy shopping bag stuffed with parcels which continually slid off her knees onto Abby each time the bus made a turn. The woman smiled apologetically the first time, but after five miles had passed, the parcels were left conveniently where they slid while the woman stared out the window. Abby edged an inch or two closer to the aisle and gritted her teeth. The bus stopped again to discharge two passengers and pick up three—all of whom had to stand in the aisle, where their dripping raincoats managed to dampen the hapless seated passengers, who had no escape.

Abby bit her lip and glanced at her watch—wishing that she'd asked how long the trip to the Maritime Museum was supposed to take. Already it was getting on toward two o'clock, and they were barely halfway.

At the next bus stop, she discovered that her estimated arrival time was going to be a lot later than even her direst fears. There were at least twenty Bermuda schoolchildren waiting to board, all of them wearing shiny wet slicker raincoats, carrying book bags, and filled with *joie de vivre*. The youngsters squeezed into the bus aisle like circus clowns emerging from a trick car in the center ring. When the bus driver would say firmly, "That's all, I can't take any more," two more six-year-olds would squeeze on, grinning at their cunning.

The bus finally lurched off, every inch of space filled with humanity—most of it damp, dripping, innocent, wide-eyed, and shouting with glee. Abby found herself with parcels on one knee and a six-year-old boy on the other. The latter didn't know he was on her lap, she discovered. He was just happy to have found something to cling to in the crowded aisle.

The children may have gotten on the bus en masse, but Abby soon discovered that they left like passengers from Noah's ark—every bus stop for the next two or three miles was faithfully visited and one or two youngsters departed with shouted good-byes to their friends. Abby eventually lost the little boy on her knee and made a quick check to see if she still had an umbrella on the floor.

Because her attention was at shoe-top level, she missed seeing that the next bus stop was also across the road from an elementary school. By then, it was raining harder than ever and the next group of children, most of them aged six to eight, surged into the bus like a group of lemmings headed for the sea. For the next few miles, she had two children parked against her knee and the parcels on the other side had become old friends.

Fifteen minutes later, when the bus lurched to another stop at a shopping center in Somerset, Abigail followed two first-graders down the aisle to the door and reeled onto the ground. The bus left and rounded a curve up the road before she remembered that her umbrella was still on the floor. "Dammit to hell!" she muttered, and rolled up the collar of her coat.

She looked around the small settlement, which consisted mainly of a food market and a restaurant with a "Closed" sign in the door. Then her eye lit on a taxi which had just pulled up across the highway. The driver got out of his car and started halfway across the road, obviously headed for the restaurant, until he noted the sign on the door.

He'd barely turned back toward the car before Abigail was flying across the roadway after him, calling, "Hey! Just a minute. Can you take a fare?"

The stocky native paused in the drizzle long enough to nod and jerk a thumb toward his car before sprinting back behind the wheel. Abby arrived an instant later and almost fell into the backseat in her relief.

"You're lucky, lady," was his opening remark. "There's a long wait for taxis out here. Where do you want to go?"

"Down by the Maritime Museum to the perfume factory, and afterward, could you take me back to Hamilton?"

He hesitated, his hand poised over the meter. "That'll run into money. There's a bus—of course, that'd take a little longer."

By dint of great self-control, Abby didn't tell him that she knew it. She also didn't mention that by then she had a speaking acquaintance with practically every schoolchild who lived in the parishes of Warwick and Southampton and she wasn't anxious to renew the friendships just then. She said firmly, "I'm on a vacation, so I can be a little extravagant. Do you know the perfume factory I'm talking about?"

He nodded and let his hand drop from the meter. "Yes, ma'am. If we're going all the way to Hamilton, you'd do better to hire me by the hour. Maybe I could show you some points of interest on the way back to town."

"If we have time, I'd like that," Abby told him, slipping off her damp shoes and wriggling in the luxury of the empty backseat. "What's the latest on the hurricane?"

The driver turned on the ignition, but took time to glance over his shoulder. "Not good—though it may take a while to get here. Just ask anybody who lives on the island."

"What do you mean?" Abby was paying close attention as he drove along the winding road, finally coming into view of the water again.

"All the spiderwebs the last day or so," the driver

said, gesturing toward the thick undergrowth beside the road. "They're a sure sign of a storm."

"I see." Abby's tone was respectful, remembering some of the homely ways that weather was forecast at home, which often proved more accurate than the latest satellite information. "Was that a ferry pier we passed back there?"

He nodded. "Watford Bridge stop. You'd have quite a wait for the return trip to Hamilton, though."

"I haven't changed my mind," Abby assured him hastily. "I was just getting my bearings if I came this way again—it's probably faster than the bus."

"And a lot safer than one of those," the man agreed as a moped buzzed by them on a dangerous curve in the road. "You'd be surprised how many tourists spend their time here in hospital."

Or on a school bus, Abby almost said as the taxi went past the bus she'd been on when it pulled into still another stop. "Is the perfume factory close to the museum?"

"Not far. Sort of a . . . what do you call it?"—he searched for the proper term and then said—"industrial complex, that's it. S'funny your wanting to go to the factory, though, because they don't encourage tourists."

She noted his dubious look at her in the rear-vision mirror and hurried to reassure him. "That's what I was told, but I'm here on business. A friend of mine gave me the name of the manager."

He nodded and trod on the accelerator again when they passed another small shopping area with a sign which read "Maritime Museum straight ahead." By then,

there was more water than land on view as they pro-
ceeded along the narrow fingers of Boaz Island and
Ireland Island South. The water of the enclosed Great
Sound was to the right, with the heavily populated
Pembroke parish and city of Hamilton just visible in the
distance. To the left of the road, there were picturesque
beaches visible behind the luxuriant greenery—looking
like miniatures on a postcard with palm trees to frame
the view. Still beyond was the endless reach of the
Atlantic, where the wind was causing havoc with the
white frothy spindrift atop ominous gray swells.

And then, abruptly, the taxi went over a slight rise.
Before them was the big dockyard area and Maritime
Museum of the former naval installation at the northwest tip of Ireland Island. The passage of years since
the Royal Navy had abandoned the premises had taken
a toll on the huge fortification, which once had enabled
the British forces to control the entire east coast of
North America—even serving to launch an assault on
Washington, D.C., during the War of 1812. Abby ob-
served crumbling stone walls and rusted metal derricks
as the car went past empty docks. She leaned forward
to say, "Are you sure the perfume factory is in here? It
looks as if everything has been forsaken for years."

The driver shook his head and took one hand off the
wheel to point toward a crowded parking area near one
of the buildings in an industrial zone. "There's plenty
still going on around here. Of course, it isn't anything
to do with the Navy anymore. Except that there's a lot
of their belongings in the museum. You could go through

there after you get finished with your business—unless it's past closing time."

"When is that?"

A troubled expression came over his face. "I'm not exactly sure. Not many of my fares come out this far," he added defensively. "Maybe I can find out while you're in the perfume factory." He slowed to negotiate a corner and then drove down between a row of two-story structures which appeared to be warehouses.

The taxi man turned into still another narrow street with a rambling old stone building at the end of it. "There's the perfume place," he told Abby in some triumph as he braked beside a small delivery van. "Is this close enough? I'd park in front of the door, except that it looks as if somebody's coming out." He jerked his head toward a mid-sized car backing from a space beyond the van as he spoke.

"This will be fine," Abby said automatically, reaching for the door. Then as she identified the driver of the other car, instinct made her slide back into the corner of the taxi seat, partially out of sight.

"Something wrong, miss?" The driver, who'd started to open his own door, threw her a concerned look.

"No. Not really," Abigail stuttered. She couldn't very well admit that it was not only the surprise of seeing Ian Woodbourne behind the wheel of the other car, but that he was chauffeuring Brian St. John and Maida Collins, who had just emerged from the perfume factory. Abby drew back even further in her corner when she saw St. John give her waiting taxi a curious look, and thanked her stars that the delivery van in between prevented a more searching inspection.

Even as she sat motionless, watching as they got in their car, she wondered why she didn't make her presence known. Certainly it would have been the ideal time to ask the gallery owner about her Burns watercolor. But her surprise at discovering such an unlikely threesome kept her immobile.

Ian revved the engine and cut sharply to get out of the small cul-de-sac, fortunately using the other side of the drive. Evidently St. John's interest in her taxi had only been momentary, because he and Maida were deep in conversation and didn't look back, even when their car stopped and turned onto the arterial at the end of the road.

Abby frowned as she tried to remember whether she'd mentioned the St. John gallery during her dinner date with Ian. She was sure that she had—just as a matter of conversation. So why hadn't he said that he knew the man? It would have been far more logical than to remain silent. Unless Ian preferred not to combine his business and social life.

"Maybe you don't feel well." It was the taxi driver again, but by then he'd gotten out of the car and had her door open, staring in at her with concern. "We could go down to the museum—there's a room where they serve tea," he said. "If it's still open. Otherwise, there's a place in Somerset—"

"No—no, I'm fine," Abby cut in apologetically. "I was just thinking of something else. Would you please wait for me? I shouldn't be long inside."

"No matter." When he'd helped her out, he slammed the door and stood leaning against the car, hunched against the drizzle. "I'll be here."

Once inside the factory, Abigail frowned as she stared around her. She hadn't expected anything like a Madison Avenue advertising-agency interior, but she had hoped to find more than two scuffed desks against the wall and some metal filing cabinets which had obviously seen better days. There was no faulting the warehouse facilities beyond, however, where corrugated cartons were piled high on wooden pallets ready for shipping. They were identified by overhead signs, designating the various fragrances. Abby wandered across the concrete floor to peep into an open carton on one of the piles.

"Sorry, miss—we don't allow visitors unless by appointment," called an English-accented voice.

Abby whirled to see a short, heavyset man with thinning fair hair coming from a door beyond the desk area. He was dressed in a violent plaid sport coat and none-too-clean gabardine trousers, but he made an attempt to straighten his tie as he bustled importantly toward her.

"If you're interested in the product, I can give you a list of our local outlets," he said, coming up beside her. He made a point of fastening the top of the open carton to emphasize his displeasure.

Abigail halfway expected him to go through her bulging purse, in case she'd helped herself to the merchandise in the interim. "Actually, I do have a kind of appointment," she told him before that could happen. "My name is Trent, and a friend of mine—Josephine

Lamont of the Evergreen retail chain—wrote that I might call on you. That is, if you're Mr. Breen?"

The man shook his head, but his attitude became more conciliating as he said, "Breen's no longer with the company. Actually, there's been a change of ownership in the last week. What was it that this friend of yours wanted?"

"Prices and delivery schedules. Mr. Breen practically promised her employers an exclusive distributorship for their territory. She also wanted me to bring back samples to cover your whole line of fragrances for a comprehensive publicity campaign. That is, if you can sell retail to me." She looked at him hopefully. "I couldn't find all the labels I needed in Hamilton."

"That's beyond my authority—the distributorship, I mean." By then, the man's blustering manner had changed completely. "I don't know what's going to happen to the company now. It's a pity you weren't a little earlier. You just missed our new owner."

"Oh?" Abigail waited expectantly, hoping that the manager would go on with his explanation.

He wasn't to be drawn. "I suppose I could let you have some of the samples," he said finally, "but your friend will have to wait for a new price quote. You can leave her name and address," he added as he went back to open the top drawer of one of the filing cabinets, where he extracted a display box containing six small bottles of perfume. "I won't charge you for these. The bottles weren't up to our usual quality, but the contents are perfectly all right."

"That's very kind of you," Abby assured him as she

wrote down Josephine's business address and phone number on a piece of paper. "I'll tell Mrs. Lamont what you said." Tucking the perfume samples under her arm, she added, "You'd better give me the name of the new owner so that she'll know whom to contact in the future."

"I'll be handling all that," the man said, drawing himself up importantly and fishing in the breast pocket of his sport coat for a card. "Just tell her to get in touch with me after a week or so and I'll see what we can do." He walked over to the door and opened it, leaving Abby no alternative but to follow.

"I won't keep you any longer, then," she said. "I hope that I haven't interrupted your busy schedule."

The manager took her words at face value. "No, no. That's what I'm paid for. Ask your friend to write for current price lists. Beast of a day, isn't it?"

The last came as he hovered with her on the threshold and took a quick look at the dark clouds. An instant later, he closed the door decisively behind her.

Abby stood, dazed, where he'd left her. It took some time for her to find any logic in what she'd just learned.

Which of the threesome in the car was the new owner of the company? Or had there been someone completely different who'd ducked out the back door? That made far more sense than any of the people she'd seen. Ian was merely a charter freight pilot and didn't appear to possess a bankroll for financing any kind of company. Maida wouldn't be working in a bird refuge with Blair if she had great financial aspirations. Which left Brian St. John. Abby frowned, and then decided that she might do a little subtle questioning about his other interests when she collected the Burns print. "So welcome to Bermuda," she muttered, and walked across the forecourt to where her taxi was waiting.

"Everything okay, miss?" The driver scrambled out to help her into the car.

"I guess so. At least as good as I expected—the way things are going today. Maybe we could take time for that cup of tea now . . . er . . ." Abby searched for the driver's license identification, usually posted by the meter, but failing to find it, added, "What *is* your name?"

"Ezekiel. Most people call me Zeke," he replied, getting back behind the wheel.

"All right, then, Zeke."

He must have noticed her questioning glance for his cab identification because he smiled, saying, "I had to send in for my annual license renewal. It takes a few days for the red tape," he confessed as he turned the car toward the end of the island. "The picture I had last year looked like a man from the police 'wanted' list."

"I think that happens on everybody's driver's license. Oh, darn!" Her exclamation came a few minutes later when they drove up to the Maritime Museum and she saw a chain stretched across the entrance. "So much for our cup of tea. Well, maybe there'll be another day."

Zeke nodded in sympathy. "We could stop at that place in Somerset—'cept it's not very good."

"Probably the best thing to do would be head back toward Hamilton," Abby said, glancing at the overcast sky. "The weather isn't getting any better. For the first time, I'm beginning to believe that storm is really coming." She stared out toward the deserted piers with the rusted fittings in the old naval yard as Zeke drove back up the hill toward the main gate. "I'd hate to be caught in this place in a high wind—the whole blooming thing could collapse. It's like a ghost town, isn't it?"

"Not much like downtown Hamilton," Zeke agreed, and then slowed when a black-and-white cat darted across the road into the shrubbery on the hillside to their left. "He won't live long at that rate. It's what happened to my cat last month. Got run down by a car right in front of my house."

"That's a shame. You get terribly attached to a family pet, I know." A sudden impulse made her say, "If you feel like having another cat, there's an orange stray roaming the hotel grounds where I'm staying. At least he was there the night before last."

Zeke's smile flashed white in his dark face. "Sounds as if you're going in the adoption business while you're here."

"I'd like to. He looked like such a nice cat, but terribly thin. It must be an orphan or the neighborhood scrounge."

"I'll think about it. When I drive you back to your hotel, maybe I can take a look at him."

Abby opened her lips to say that she hadn't planned on going back there just then, but decided against it. There was still a little time before dusk, and there was no reason Zeke couldn't drive her to Blair's apartment after their search for the cat. It was probably crazy, she knew, but it made as much sense as anything that had happened. She took a deep breath and said, "Fair enough. If that cat knows what's good for him, he'll be at the hotel waiting for us under the nearest palm tree."

Chapter Seven

Despite her hopes and Zeke's, too, when they finally parked in the lot at the hotel and made a search of the grounds, the marmalade cat remained stubbornly out of sight.

"Wouldn't you know!" Abby fretted. She was trying to ignore her soaking feet after trudging around the wet grass, peering under shrubbery and up palm trunks. "Just like a fool cat! Missing such a wonderful chance!"

Zeke turned up the collar of his plastic rain jacket and nodded. "You've got me curious, so I won't give up. Maybe tomorrow would be better, though. No cat with any sense would be out in this rain."

"Of course. I should have realized." Abby started back for the hotel path, trying to ignore the squishing sound of her shoes as she walked. "It was nice of you to come looking. Now, if you'd take me back to that apartment-hotel we passed on the way here, I'll call it a day."

If Zeke harbored any curiosity as to why she was dividing her time between two hotels just a few blocks apart, he was smart enough to remain quiet about it, and nodded agreeably.

Abby paid him off in front of Blair's apartment-hotel a few minutes later, adding a hefty tip which had his smile stretching from ear to ear.

As she let herself in the building, there was an elderly woman dressed in a black uniform emptying ashtrays in the office area. She looked up as Abigail crossed to the stairway, nodding in response to a murmured greeting. Abby didn't linger for any conversation because she'd caught sight of the foyer clock and winced as she saw the hour.

Blair yanked open the door as soon as she touched the keyhole. "Where in the devil have you been?" he growled, making no attempt to lower his voice even though a couple was just emerging from a room down the corridor. A flush did darken his cheekbones when the two people passed on their way to the stairs, not hiding their interest in the proceedings. Blair put a heavy hand at Abigail's elbow and propelled her into the living room. He shut the door behind them and raked her with a baleful glance. "I can't tell whether you do it deliberately or whether you haven't got the sense you were born with."

She sank onto the davenport, suddenly exhausted after her long afternoon. "Your grammar's atrocious," she informed him, "and so are your manners. At least I don't have to worry about my reputation here after that touching reception." She broke off to stare hopefully at him. "Or did you do it on purpose?"

"If I'd done what I wanted to do, I'd have turned you over my knee and whaled—"

"—the living daylights out of me." She stared incredulously at a velvet cushion with 'Souvenir of Bermuda' stitched across it before putting it behind her head. "Your reaction's about as out-of-date as the decor in this place."

Blair's eyes were narrow slits as he walked across the room to stand in front of her. "So I'm old-fashioned," he said in a tone that was all the more ominous because he didn't raise his voice. "I can still handle you without any trouble, and don't you forget it. And if that means keeping you tied up in the bedroom with a 'Do Not Disturb' sign on the door—I'll damned well do it. There's too much at stake for you to be tripping through the tulips and making one hell of a mess out of all our efforts in the process."

Abigail swallowed and drew back instinctively as he brought his hands up, and then felt foolish when he simply crossed his arms on his chest, still towering over her.

"Do I make myself clear?" he rapped out after she didn't respond.

"Of course. You don't have to spell it out."

"Then why in the devil weren't you around anytime when I tried to reach you today? I made a special trip back here, and there wasn't even a note so I'd know where to start searching."

"I wasn't lost," Abby pointed out, feeling a trifle guilty when she realized that a good part of his anger was thinly disguised concern. Even so, she rationalized, he didn't have to treat her like a thoughtless adolescent. "And I certainly wasn't alone," she went on defiantly. "In fact, I spent over an hour with half the school kids in Bermuda. Right smack in the middle of them," she said, her voice rising as she remembered. "My feet haven't been dry since."

"Damned if I can see any connection between school kids and your showing up here like a soggy crumpet. Why don't you get out of those clothes before you end up with pneumonia along with everything else?"

"If you'd give me a chance, I could tell you about the connection," she lashed back, ignoring his last remark. "All you do is stand there like a . . . a . . . cigar-store Indian and make cutting remarks."

As soon as the words were out, she realized that her description left a lot to be desired. Blair must have thought so too, because his brows went up in amusement. "Maybe you should try that one again."

"I thought you wanted me to get changed."

"You're right, I do." He waved an arm in the direction of the bedroom and then frowned as he saw her pick up her package with the perfume samples. "Don't the stores in Hamilton wrap things anymore?"

She looked down at the small package and wondered if Blair's suspicion could possibly be caused by jealousy. "Actually, I didn't buy these," she confessed, deciding to put her theory to the test. "They were a present."

"Not Ian, was it?"

Abby leaned against the doorjamb, her expression innocent. "Heavens no! I didn't see him today. I mean, not officially."

"Very amusing. That is, if you have a warped sense of humor, but it's late and frankly I'd like to go out for dinner before midnight."

"Will you listen to me?" she cut in, sorry that she'd followed her perverse impulse. Especially when she saw how weary Blair looked in the dim overhead light—as if he hadn't slept properly for a week. "I just saw Ian in another car when he drove by," she explained. "He wasn't the reason I was late. That was because I asked Zeke to detour by the hotel grounds so he could see that stray cat."

"Zeke who?" The words came out like ice chips.

"I don't know," Abby said, looking blank. "It didn't occur to me to ask. He's a cab driver who picked me up out by the end of the bus line in Somerset."

Blair's forehead smoothed miraculously. "You mean Ezekiel?"

"I guess so." It was Abby who frowned then in sudden suspicion. "You know him?"

"I've heard about him. He's one of the more popular fellows here on the island. There was a piece about him in the paper a while back. Don't tell me that you got him to adopt that orange stray of yours?"

"I wish I could, but we couldn't find him. That's how I got so wet—tramping around the grass by the pool." She saw him open his mouth, and cut him off. "I know. Go get changed. Give me ten minutes, or are we going someplace salubrious?"

"Sorry. Not this time." Blair shot a look at his watch. "We'd better stay in the neighborhood for dinner. There's a Chinese place down the block that's not bad. Is that okay?"

Abby wanted to ask him what the tremendous hurry was, but after her earlier fiasco decided it wasn't the time. She nodded and went in the bedroom to change, wishing that she'd brought more of her wardrobe when she'd left the other hotel.

Blair didn't find anything wrong with her cream silk blouse and burgundy velveteen skirt when she reappeared a little later. His only comment beyond a crooked smile of approval was, "Can you wear a raincoat over that? The restaurant's just a ways down the street, so it doesn't make much sense to use the car."

She nodded and watched him shrug into a poplin raincoat before helping her into the topcoat she'd left on a Victorian coatrack behind the door.

"You'll need something for your hair unless you can outrun the drizzle," he said, buttoning her up with calm expertise and standing back to survey the finished result.

She pulled a scarf out of her pocket and tied it over her head. "Next you'll be asking where my mittens are."

He grinned at her gentle chiding. "I knew I forgot something."

There wasn't any more conversation as they made their way through the rain gusts across the street and down to the end of the block, arriving finally at a garishly decorated Chinese restaurant.

"It looks awfully quiet tonight," Blair muttered as he held the door for her and they went into a dimly lit foyer. "This place changed management a couple weeks ago. I hope they didn't change cooks at the same time."

"It'll be fine," Abby reassured him as she saw a young Oriental in a white waiter's coat stroll their way from the back of the restaurant. "Chinese food is the safest thing in town. It's hard to go wrong there."

"Maybe. But this could be the exception." Blair urged her ahead of him when the waiter beckoned to a shadowy booth in the rear. "We'll soon find out."

Except that it wasn't soon. They discovered that when they ordered pork chow mein—to be on the safe side—and had almost drained the entire pot of tea which came with the menu before their entrée arrived.

The food was slapped down in front of them by the reluctant waiter, who disappeared as they were still staring at the dishes in consternation.

"What was that you said about not being able to go wrong with Chinese food?" Blair asked grimly after taking the first bite.

"Well . . ." Abby drew the word out as she tried to think of something charitable to say about the concoction in front of her. "There are lots of vegetables—maybe it's Cantonese style."

"Or Northwest Hamilton," Blair said, chewing on a tough piece of celery.

"Or 'Cook's Night Out,' " Abby confirmed, unable to subdue a giggle. "This isn't so bad if you think of it as the vegetarian plate."

Blair gave an inelegant snort, showing what he thought of that idea, and looked at his watch again. "Unfortunately, it's too late for dinner at any place around here." His gaze came up to meet Abby's. "A few more vacations like this and you'll never leave home again. At least you fared better with your fly-boy last night."

"Ian?" She gestured airily with her fork, having decided after the first bite that trying to cope with chopsticks as well as the food would really bring on indigestion. "He's not any particular friend of mine. I must say that I was surprised to see him with your chum out at the perfume factory today." She swallowed a bit of bamboo shoot before adding, "Of course, he *did* say he'd been flying in here for some time."

"Wait a minute." Blair had his cup of tea halfway to his lips but he put it back down on the table again as he stared at her. "Start again and sort it out. What chum of mine are you talking about?"

"Maida. I thought you knew. The three of them were out at the factory and drove off together."

"Three?"

"The third one was Brian St. John. Oh, Lord!" Her hand came up to her lips in dismay. "I never did get around to calling the gallery again this afternoon. Well, he probably didn't go back to the place. Especially if he's worrying about his new investment." Blair's only reaction to that bit of information was another irritated snort, and Abby looked across the table to see him close his eyes, as if annoyed beyond measure. "What's the matter? Did you hit a bad noodle?"

"You could say that." Blair's eyes opened again. "What investment?"

"I beg your pardon?"

"The one that St. John is pursuing."

"Oh, that. I'm just guessing. . . ." She took time for a

sip of tea and almost choked as Blair's palm came down hard on the table beside his plate. "What are you doing?" she gasped. "Good Lord, what will people think?"

"There aren't any 'people,'" he said in a goaded voice. "We're the only customers—with good reason. Get on with your story, for God's sake. I'm late as it is."

"Then why don't we skip the whole thing . . ."

"Abigail!"

She looked distinctly nervous at his muted roar and saw that even the waiter deigned to give them a look from his stool by the door. Reluctantly she said, "I meant the perfume factory—if you must know. The manager said the new owner had just left. So it must have been St. John—unless your friend Maida has come into money. Lots of money, I should think. That place is a going concern, because they do business all over the world." Abby took another sip of tea and added reflectively, "That must mean that St. John is the owner—he's the only one with that much money. After all, if he has his gallery storeroom stuffed with Kenneth Burns originals, he can't be on a very strict budget."

Blair looked like a man who'd missed the first act of the play and was trying to catch up. "Slow down, will you. What's all this about Burns originals?"

"I saw them when I visited the gallery the other day. He probably paid a mint to get that many from the artist's estate. I must say, he wasn't happy when he found me looking them over from the doorway. He practically bit my head off and then shoved me back downstairs."

"I'll be damned." Blair spoke almost under his breath, his eyes fixed on the tablecloth in front of him.

Abby thought she was missing something and followed his glance but failed to see anything other than a few errant splashes of soy sauce from an earlier meal. "Is there something wrong?" she asked finally. "Am I boring you? More than usual." The last had a bitter tinge.

He blinked and looked up, making an effort to sound convincing. "Certainly not." He raised his hand and flagged the waiter with a gesture that was impossible for even that young man to ignore.

He came over and peered at their far-from-empty dishes. "You want something?"

"Just the check," Blair said tersely. "And right away, please."

When the check arrived in solitary splendor on a greasy plate, Abby complained mildly, "Not even a fortune cookie."

Blair didn't pause in reaching for his wallet. "You should have mentioned them before."

"I know that—now. Never mind."

"Probably you wouldn't have liked the fortunes inside, if they're anything like the rest of the menu. Don't fret. I'll buy you a whole bagful some other time," he promised, putting money down to cover the bill and the tip. "Got your coat? Let's go, then."

Abigail hesitated once they were outside the restaurant door, reluctant to plunge into the drizzle. Then her lips curved in a smile. "Your place or mine?"

Blair's eyebrows rose. "I'll bet you've been waiting all

night to get that phrase in. Mine, of course. I don't want you back in that other hotel except for checking out tomorrow."

"Checking out!" She tried to hold back as he marched her down the sidewalk, but his grip on her elbow made it impossible to slacken her pace. "Just a darned minute!" She pulled out of his clasp and stood stubbornly in the middle of the deserted sidewalk. "What are you talking about? Why should I check out? I've practically just arrived."

"But you're practically on your way home." He put a hand in the middle of her back to propel her on her way again, but more gently this time. "That latest storm in the Caribbean has made up its mind. The weather service is now saying that it will hit Bermuda tomorrow night. It's supposed to reach the Bahamas in the early morning." He stiffened to shelter her from a burst of wind that flattened the shrubbery beside them against a brick retaining wall. "Jonas doesn't want you here in a hurricane, and neither do I."

His sudden ultimatum left her openmouthed. "But there isn't a prayer of getting on a flight—every tourist in town will be trying to do the same thing."

Blair didn't slacken his pace until they turned into the brick-enclosed patio of his building, which afforded partial protection from the rain squalls. "I'm not talking about planes. The purser of the *Southern Cross*—that big cruise ship anchored at the midtown pier—is a friend of mine. They had an empty stateroom, but only because one of their passengers lives in Bermuda and didn't buy the entire cruise. All you have to do is be aboard by one o'clock tomorrow. It's a good idea to check in earlier in case their sailing time is moved up. The captain doesn't plan to be tied up to a dock in Hamilton if hurricane winds hit the island."

"I should think that's just where he'd like to be."

Blair grinned. "He's worried about the ship—not the passengers' digestions—and it's better to be at sea in a case like this. Don't worry, the shipping company knows what to do."

"But what about you?"

"I still have a job here." Blair shoved back his cuff and groaned slightly as he saw the time. "I'll have to go."

"Will you be back? To sleep, I mean. Surely you can't be expected to work day and night." Abigail tacked on the last after his glance lingered on her flushed cheeks.

Blair urged her farther under the shelter to escape the rain. His hand came up to push a strand of her hair gently behind her ear. "That sounds more like wife-talk than a temporary roommate. Maybe the humidity here on the island is softening that independence of yours."

"That's ridiculous!" Abby pushed his hand away from the curve of her cheek and immediately missed the touch of his lean fingers. Only a fool would put any importance on such an absentminded fondling, she told herself. Especially when he'd already arranged to get her out of town.

"I'll try to be quiet when I get back," he was going on, "but don't do anything silly like waiting up for me.

You'll need a good night's rest, considering what's in store tomorrow."

Abby yanked off her head scarf, blinking through sudden tears as she reached for the doorknob. Here she'd been putting romantic thoughts in his mind and he wasn't even coming up with her to check the apartment. For that, he could certainly spend the night on the davenport again when he finally *did* get home— despite the fact that she'd planned to occupy it herself and give him the bedroom.

Blair stopped her halfway through the door. "What's the matter, Abby? That dinner didn't get to you, did it?"

"Of course not." She managed to slide away from him, lingering only to ask over her shoulder. "Will I see you in the morning?"

"I don't know. Don't worry, we'll make sure that you get safely on the ship." He grinned and turned up his raincoat collar. "Jonas will be glad to hear that you're showing so much sense."

She should have found his last words comforting. Abby told herself that over and over when she reached the deserted apartment and determinedly got into her nightgown and robe. She relented enough to fix Blair's makeshift bed on the couch, but didn't waste any time in going back in the bedroom and closing the door behind her. After that, she walked over to the window and rested her forehead against the cool glass, her insides feeling as turbulent as the jerking silhouettes of the shrubbery below when it reacted to the strong gusts of wind.

She took a deep unhappy breath and told herself it was simply indigestion from that horrible dinner—wishing that she could believe it. If she had any sense she'd go to bed and get a decent night's sleep as Blair had ordered—because at this time tomorrow night she'd probably still be unhappy with her love life and seasick to boot!

Chapter Eight

Abby opened her eyes the next morning to the sound of rain still beating against the window and a gray sky overcast with clouds so thick they looked as if they'd arrived to spend a month or two. Probably they'd blown in from Nassau as a forerunner of things to come.

It was almost eerily quiet in the living room and Abigail wasn't surprised to find it empty when she peered around the door. She frowned as she noticed that the bedding on the couch hadn't been touched, and then her frown deepened as she saw a half-empty cup on the kitchen counter which definitely hadn't been there when she'd gone to bed.

Blair must have come in during the night or early morning and stayed just long enough to make himself a cup of coffee.

"Oh, hell!" Abby said distinctly, and put on some water to see if coffee would help in her case.

She folded the bedding and put it away first so that the maid wouldn't have any additional tidbits for gossip. After she'd finished, she spooned instant coffee into a mug, reflecting how strange to be protecting Blair's good name at that point.

She turned on the radio for a weather report to go with her coffee. The first words confirmed that Bermuda was in the track of the hurricane coming from the Bahamas. The announcement tersely cited the storm's present rate of progress and said the high winds were expected to hit Hamilton by evening.

Abby held her head for a moment and then went over to phone the steamship line as Blair had ordered. It took a while to get through, but when she reached the passenger agent, she was told to be aboard by noon at the latest.

"I'd suggest that you keep checking with us, Miss Trent," the man went on in a clipped British accent. "Sailing time could be moved up with very little notice. We'll do our best to reach passengers ashore, but naturally it's your responsibility."

"So I gather," Abby said dryly, remembering the small print on steamship tickets she'd seen on other occasions. "It sounds like a rough sailing."

"That's what the captain is trying to avoid, Miss Trent," she was told with some asperity. "You're fortunate to have a cabin—you wouldn't believe how many people there are who'd like to sail on this trip."

"I'm sure you're right." Abigail rang off, after meekly promising to keep in touch. She got dressed, wondering how such a splendid vacation could have turned into an utter, flat-out failure.

At least she could get her Burns print during the forenoon, she told herself, while struggling into her coat and tying on a head scarf against the weather. Before leaving she tried the St. John gallery and heard the phone ringing without answer. She put down the receiver with more force than necessary, thinking unkind thoughts about people who didn't believe in early shop hours.

She was halfway out the door before she felt a twinge of conscience and came back to leave a note for Blair on the kitchen counter telling that she'd be back by eleven at the latest. For an instant, she thought about saying that she was on her way to the gallery in St. George and then decided it wasn't necessary. He couldn't possibly object to a public bus ride and there were bound to be plenty of people around when she got off in the middle of the popular tourist attraction.

Determined not to waste any more time, she took a cruising taxi up to the main square, where she boarded a waiting bus. She was happy to see that, this time, there wasn't a schoolchild in sight as they pulled out toward the North Shore Road. Only then did she remember the radio broadcast mentioning that all schools in the vicinity would be closed until the emergency passed.

The weather wasn't making a drastic change in most people's way of life, she decided as the bus rolled imperturbably from stop to stop—picking up cheerful villagers loaded with groceries who were trying to manage their packages and stow away dripping umbrellas at the same time. Most of the conversations were about the impending storm, but there wasn't any alarm, Abby noted. Rather a calm resignation and acceptance of what was in store.

As the bus passed Flatts Bridge, she saw a crew of men putting up shutters on one of the bigger tourist villas while still other workmen were battening down everything possible in the nearby marina filled with pleasure craft.

The boats made Abby think of the liner she was due to board in a few hours and she felt a twinge of uneasiness that she had so many things left to do. Assembling her belongings from both hotels would take time, and so would the actual checking out. Especially if Blair weren't around when she returned from St. George and she waited to say good-bye.

A different rumble from the roadway made her glance out of the bus window to see that they were going over the long causeway constructed of coral which connected St. George's and Kindley Field to the main island. At least it wouldn't be much longer until she found out if Brian St. John had fulfilled his promise with the Burns print.

When they pulled into the outskirts of the charming old town of St. George a little later, the sidewalks were almost bereft of people—unlike the usual busy appearance when cruise liners were at anchor. The explanation came as her bus driver let off the rest of his passengers at a main stop on Duke of York street.

"This place'll be like a ghost town pretty soon," he

announced with a wave of his arm. "Those two ships that were here last night cut short their stay and headed for sea first thing this morning. The word's out that they didn't even wait to get all their passengers back from shore trips. The company will put 'em up at a hotel here, but some of the folks are pretty hot under the collar. They'll sure have a story to tell when they finally get home again."

"*If* they get home," muttered the man getting off in front of Abby. "At least the wind's let up a little."

Abby pulled the belt of her coat tighter and looked around, trying to remember her directions. Just behind her was Old Maid's Lane, and Silk Alley was ahead. If she remembered right, the gallery was two blocks down— just beyond the church.

She walked steadily toward it. Already many of the attractive shop windows facing the narrow sidewalk were either shuttered or barricaded as a precaution against the coming storm. One of the inns across the street was doing a rousing business, which indicated townsfolk had decided to ease their worries in congenial company.

A different sort of sound coming down the steep steps from the old church made her pull up with a bemused expression. That wasn't just choir practice she was hearing, but a choir accompanied by the soft, lilting tones of handbells. She was sure of it!

She risked a quick look at her watch and decided that another five minutes or so wouldn't matter—a chance to watch accomplished handbell ringers was too good to miss. Now, if only it weren't a closed rehearsal, she thought as she hurried up the church's steep steps. It was surprising not to find the vicar or the sexton out putting shutters over the stained-glass windows. Maybe they reasoned that if a building had been around for more than two centuries, a rumored hurricane wasn't cause for panic.

Abigail hesitated at the top of the stairs, but her heartbeat accelerated again when she heard hurried footsteps behind her. Her elbow was caught in a firm grasp before she could turn and see what was happening.

"Abby! I thought it was you!" Ian pulled up beside her, breathing hard. "You lead a merry chase, love."

"And you just about scared me to death," she told him wryly. Then, noting that he was in a dark gray uniform with wings over the pocket, she said, "What's all the excitement? Are you about to beat the hurricane out, too?"

His fair eyebrows climbed. "So you did plan to leave without letting me know?"

"Actually, I haven't had any spare time lately."

"I see. Well, you certainly didn't waste any of it in your room at the hotel," he said accusingly. "I've been trying to get you ever since yesterday afternoon. That *was* you skulking in the back of that cab out by the Maritime Museum earlier, wasn't it?"

"I didn't think you saw me," Abigail replied, annoyed to find herself on the defensive. "Besides, you were busy and I didn't want to bother you." She suddenly became aware that the music from the church had stopped, and she frowned. "I hope I haven't missed out completely."

"Missed what?"

"The rehearsal," she replied, wondering if he held a minor inquisition with all of his dinner dates or whether he was just annoyed at having been seen with another woman. If Maida *was* the reason, it was certainly time to set him right. "Look, Ian, it's been great meeting you . . ."

"But . . ."

"I beg your pardon?"

"That was the next word, wasn't it? It was great to see me, but right now you have other things to do." His hand tightened on her elbow and he urged her forward, around the front of the church on a brick-lined walk. "That's what I want to talk about—those other things. First of all, let's find a little privacy. This should serve nicely."

"But I don't want to look at the garden—as pretty as it is," Abigail added hastily after a quick glance around the secluded patio area where the enclosing coral walls were almost obscured by pink bougainvillea. "I wanted to watch the bell-ringers inside."

An unbelieving frown creased Ian's narrow forehead as he stared at her. "Are you telling me that's what brought you out here this morning?"

"I don't know where you get such silly ideas." She gestured toward the church. "I wasn't aware they were having a bell-ringing rehearsal until I walked by."

He shoved his hands in his pockets and stared at her consideringly. "Then what *are* you doing in St. George?"

"If you must know . . ." She broke off then, her head tilted at a defiant angle. "I really can't see what business it is of yours."

Her off-putting tone brought a wash of color to his face. "Don't be daft!" he snapped back. "It's a bit late in the game for any more maneuvering. I don't know what they used to get you here, but you'd have been smarter to stay away."

Her lips parted. "What in the world are you talking about?"

"Don't bother denying it. Next you'll claim that you weren't headed for the gallery."

"That's ridiculous. As a matter of fact, it's the only reason I came to St. George."

"So join the crowd." Ian's crooked smile was merely a gesture; his glance didn't contain a vestige of humor as he kept it riveted on her face. "It was fortunate for me that you were a little late."

All at once Abby became aware how very quiet and deserted the garden patio was on that early autumn day. There wasn't even any wind to stir the heavy shrubbery, cut off as it was behind the main church building and totally enclosed elsewhere by the high walls. There were some neatly kept flowerbeds full of blooming hibiscus and iron benches on the two winding walks, but for any practical purpose, she might as well have been on an outer island in the Great Sound.

Some instinct warned her to keep such disquieting thoughts from Ian. She took a deep breath to calm her rioting imagination and said in a level voice, "I don't know why you're so unhappy with me, but let's forget the whole thing. You must be on a tight schedule, too, so we might as well . . ."

"Shake hands? Or were you going to suggest a friendly

good-bye kiss?" Ian let out a sudden bark of laughter and caught her wrist to pull her close. "I've a much better idea. Not that your friend Blair will appreciate it."

"What does he have to do with all this? He doesn't even know I'm here."

Ian's expression changed to smug satisfaction and she realized that she'd unwittingly played right into his hands. His next words confirmed it. "That's even better than I'd hoped. Look, Abigail, we might as well sit down and talk this over like civilized people." Without ceremony, he pushed her onto the nearest garden bench, sitting down beside her to make sure she stayed there. "I'm flying out of Kindley in a half-hour, headed for an island in the Caribbean that possesses everything a person could want."

"How does that concern me?"

"Well, old thing—it's this way." He used the light confidential tone that had seemed so charming when they'd first met. "You're going to be my insurance for clearance out, in case things get sticky at the field. We may not have any trouble at all. It depends on how much that fool St. John has ratted to your friend Morley."

"You mean that Blair's here in St. George, too?"

Ian's lips thinned to an irritable line. "Don't bother with the innocent act any longer. We haven't time. Besides, you'd have trouble convincing me after you showed up at the factory yesterday." He shifted but kept his grip on her wrist. "I'm surprised that Morley dragged you into this business. He should have known better than to try to throw us off guard with such an obvious move."

She stared at him, bewildered. "Blair didn't have anything to do with my coming to Bermuda. Not really."

Try as she might, Abby couldn't put the required conviction in her voice for that announcement. She had pretended otherwise to her uncle and attempted to camouflage her true reasons when she'd arrived, but in her heart she knew very well that Blair's presence had drawn her like a magnet.

Now, it seemed, her denial didn't even convince Ian. Not if that derisive expression on his face was to be believed. "Try it again—this time with feeling," he mimicked. "They should have given you better training before dropping you into a major operation. God knows, we gave you plenty of warning right off."

Her eyes widened as his last words registered. "You mean that man in the gardens—out by the pool?"

Ian shrugged. "You weren't hurt. Morley appeared on the scene faster than we'd planned. That's when we suspected that he was more than the casual acquaintance you claimed."

Abby ignored that, her mind going back to the other near-disasters that had plagued her. "And the phantom knocks at my door? Or the search of my belongings while I was out with you? Were they all part of your scheme?"

Ian grimaced, plainly annoyed by her questions. "I'm not here to give you a game plan. Besides, I told you to skip that innocent touch. Your friend Blair managed to get around Maida, but once you'd arrived it didn't take me long to set her straight about his real reason for being in Bermuda. Maida doesn't like competition, and when you set up housekeeping in Morley's digs, she started breathing fire."

"Then she certainly wouldn't approve of your taking me to the Caribbean. It would just make more trouble, I'd think."

"You can stop thinking." Ian's shoulders squared belligerently under his uniform coat. "Maida doesn't make any decisions in this operation—she follows orders. And as far as anything personal, she's not my type. We decided that early on. Until Morley came on the scene, she concentrated on St. John."

"I see." Abigail swallowed uncomfortably. "And Mr. St. John's at the gallery with Blair now?"

Ian's mouth was a grim line. "I told you so, didn't I? Brian damned well better keep mum long enough to see me out of this place. He's been well paid and he knows the drill. He won't say a word without his legal adviser by his side. Besides, he hasn't been told enough to be any danger to the overall scheme. I've found out that it's safest to handle things yourself. Probably we won't have any trouble getting away at all." He surveyed her stricken face with apparent calm. "I guarantee you'll like my island hideaway, though we shouldn't have to stay there long. In a business like mine . . ." He broke off as the sound of organ music swelled into the garden from the church. Getting to his feet, he pulled her up with him. "We'd best go. I don't believe in pressing my luck."

"You can't seriously think that I'd go anyplace with you." Abby's voice wobbled despite efforts to sound adamant. "I'll scream this place down if you don't let go of me!"

"The bloody hell you will!" Ian snarled, grabbing her throat and exerting a painful pressure—enough so that she clawed at his grip to be able to breathe. "Now, behave yourself and walk out of here with me," he ordered. "Otherwise . . ." He applied even more pressure and watched with cruel satisfaction as she sagged against him. Only then did he lift his thumbs so she could drag air into her lungs with an agonizing effort. "Use your head," he went on tersely. "There's no reason we can't make this agreeable to both of us. After we get away from here . . ." He stopped, scowling, as he saw a native couple come around the corner of the church accompanied by an elderly man wearing a curate's robe. "Don't try anything," Ian warned Abby in a savage undertone. "Not if you want to live to see the sun come up tomorrow." His hand lingered by her throat in a seemingly affectionate pose as he urged her toward the street. "Just keep it easy," he said when they neared the man and woman, who were intent on what the curate was telling them.

It was something about the history of the garden, Abby gathered, hearing some of the gray-haired man's words when they came up to them. If only she knew what to do, she thought frantically, aware that her entire future depended on the next few seconds.

Ian's hand tightened on the soft flesh of her throat,

even as his voice purred in her ear, "Walk, damn you! Straight ahead!"

Abby's gait faltered as her wide-eyed gaze focused on the visitor, a neatly dressed man in a dark gray suit who glanced over his shoulder and nodded agreeably. It couldn't be—but it was! Zeke, her cab driver from the day before, who looked like a sedate member of the congregation as he and the middle-aged woman at his side moved politely, allowing Ian and Abby to pass.

It came as a distinct shock when Zeke's woman companion suddenly fell toward them, her ankle twisting on the path. Zeke, without a word, shifted his thick body to come between Abby and Ian, brushing the pilot's hand away while Ian was struggling to free himself from the other woman's devastating weight. She clung to him stubbornly, trying to regain her balance.

At the same time, Abby found herself being wrestled toward the street by the gray-haired curate. "This way, please!" His words still held a courtly manner, but there wasn't a wasted motion as he propelled her around the building—away from the sounds of a violent scuffle and shouted oaths.

And then suddenly there was a very different figure beside her after Blair stormed up the church steps three at a time.

"What are you doing here?" was all Abby could ask weakly as he clutched her.

He opened his mouth and made a strangled noise in his throat, finally closing his eyes. An instant later, they were open again and he was staring balefully down at her. "My God, that remark takes the cake! And from you—of *all* people. With nineteen square miles on this island, did you have to be in the one place that you were damned well told to stay away from?"

She stared back at him, well aware that the stiffening in her knees was dissolving as reaction set in. Then she felt Blair's none-too-gentle hand in the middle of her back, moving her to one side of the steps as four uniformed men came hurrying up, passing them with hardly a glance.

Except for one, Abby noticed belatedly. He lingered long enough to nod at Blair, jerking his thumb toward a car pulling up at the curb below.

"Right," Blair said in some satisfaction, and steered Abby toward the street.

"Wait a minute! What's all this about?" Abby tried to slow him down as they headed for the unmarked sedan where a driver sat waiting. "You've got to let me tell you about Ian . . ." she added, digging in her heels on the sidewalk as Blair opened the car door to usher her inside.

"We know all we need to about Woodbourne now." Blair's tone was scathing. "Next time you pick somebody up on a vacation, find out a little more about him. That scaly specimen turned out to be in every illegal racket he could get his hands on."

"Thank heavens they aren't going to let him go!" she said in relief. "He was scheduled to fly out in a little while and had the crazy idea of taking me with him."

"Which he might have gotten away with if Zeke hadn't seen the two of you on the church steps," Blair said with ominous finality. "You managed to leave the apartment without anybody following you this morning, although I'm blessed if I know how. Zeke was reporting to our gallery stake-out, otherwise God knows what could have happened to you. But there isn't time to go over this now." The last came as he gave a harried glance at his watch and urged her into the car. "Pack your belongings and get on that ship. The last I heard, they've moved up the sailing time."

"But what about you?" Abby wailed, frantically rolling down the car window as Blair closed the door. "When will I see you?"

There was a glittering flash of devilment in his gray eyes as he surveyed her. "I didn't think it made any difference."

"Well . . . I *would* like to hear . . ." She bit her lip as she tried to find a logical albeit untruthful reason for seeing him again. ". . . what finally happens," she finished weakly.

"Right." He sounded brisk as he straightened. "In that case, I'll make sure that you get a full report."

His nod of confirmation was all the driver was waiting for. The car was halfway down the block before Abigail could turn around and look out the rear window.

By then, Blair had disappeared from sight. Probably without giving her another thought, she concluded, and settled dejectedly back in her seat.

Chapter Nine

"I'm glad that you didn't cut it any finer, Miss Trent."

The purser's tone was jovial but there was no mistaking his words as he handed over her stateroom key and gestured for one of the young stewards to handle her baggage. "The gangway's coming up in ten minutes. I'm afraid there are going to be a lot of unhappy passengers on our trip back. They'd planned two more days' activities ashore. We'll have to make it up, one way or another."

Abby smiled slightly as she gathered her coat over her arm and zipped her purse. "Let's hope that the weather cooperates, too. Is there any chance of that hurricane changing course and following when we get out to sea?"

"We'll keep a close watch." He smiled teasingly. "We've just repainted the hull and the captain doesn't want any scratches on it when we pull into port. Now, enjoy your trip. Your bedroom steward should be on duty if you need anything in your stateroom."

Abigail nodded and followed the young crewman who carried her luggage up a wide carpeted stairway. There were throngs of people at the rail as they passed the promenade deck. From what she could see, the passengers were intent on watching the final moments of shipboard drama before the liner sailed.

"All visitors ashore, all visitors ashore," boomed a voice from the public-address speakers. "The *Southern Cross* will sail for New York in ten minutes' time. Any visitors must now leave immediately by the crew gangway forward on C Deck."

Ten minutes, Abby thought despairingly. That meant Blair couldn't see her off unless he performed miracles in getting from one end of Bermuda to the other. She hadn't wasted a minute after being driven back from St. George; the driver had even kept the car running while she'd collected her belongings at Blair's apartment before going on to the hotel. Once there, she'd found her old room to be cold and unwelcoming. She hastily stuffed her things into her big suitcase and gave a final look around. It was hard to believe that she and Blair had ever spent a night there—that she'd glanced down from that balcony to watch a marmalade tomcat frisk around the shrubbery. The cat had disappeared; the grounds were damp and uninviting—like the gray storm clouds above. Memories were made only to be forgotten, she thought sadly, and tried to put them from her mind as she fastened her luggage.

Checking out at the main desk hadn't taken long

either and the reservation clerk nodded understandingly when she asked for her bill. Even news of the impending storm had wreaked havoc in the hotel business, since there was a steady stream of departing guests.

Nearly all of them were headed for the airport, Abby discovered as her driver took her down Front Street toward the main docks. The thoroughfare was still bumper to bumper with traffic, but most of it was the moped variety or family cars loaded with natives and provisions.

A burly crew member took her luggage from the driver at the dock customs area, barely allowing Abby time to be shepherded up the gangway and directed to the purser's desk amidships.

Everybody on the darned ship seemed to be hurrying, she thought, trying to stay on the heels of the young steward as he went down a narrow corridor of the Sun Deck, finally turning into a short companionway and opening a stateroom door at the end of it. He ushered her inside and brought her things in afterward, stacking the luggage by a metal closet door. He was gone with a polite nod before Abigail could find her wallet to tip him.

She bit her lip, and then realized that she had plenty of time to correct her mistake; it would be three days before they docked in New York, since they were taking an evasive course to escape the storm. Three full days, she thought sorrowfully, and stared through a porthole into the harbor.

There was a tugboat maneuvering into position alongside the *Southern Cross* to pull the liner from her berth, but even that wasn't enough to hold her interest.

She turned back to survey the stateroom and, instead of thanking her stars that she'd landed in such pleasant surroundings, she was only aware that she was leaving Blair behind, without knowing when she'd see him again. For an instant she was tempted to make a dash for C Deck and the crew gangway, but then she heard the vibration of the ship's engines and realized it was too late for such dramatics.

Which was probably all for the best, she told herself. Undoubtedly for the best. If Blair wanted to find her, he could get in touch with Jonas. Even modern, liberated women didn't pursue a free-thinking male, she mused. Not if they wanted more than a brief affair.

That moment of truth brought her back to reality and she walked over to hang her coat in the closet which separated the main part of the stateroom with its twin beds and dressing table from the compact bathroom to her right. She poked her head in there, nodded approvingly at the immaculate white tile, and frowned slightly at the shower with its white canvas curtain. "Compact" was a charitable way to describe that shower stall, she decided. Looking at it optimistically, at least she wouldn't have far to fall if the weather got rough. It was just a good thing she wasn't any larger, she told herself.

Unbidden, her thoughts went back to Blair's tall form. With disturbing clarity she recalled the way he'd looked in his robe that night at his apartment—his broad shoulders, the smooth tanned skin that she'd tried so hard not to notice, even the way he moved . . . She drew in her breath sharply then and rested her forehead against the metal frame of the shower. Dear Lord! If she kept on at that rate, they'd take her off the ship in a padded van once they reached New York.

Which was precisely the reason she was *not* going to hang around her stateroom like a zombie, she told herself, and went back in the other room to get her purse and a jacket.

The diminutive Oriental room steward knocked while she was buttoning it and stood smiling in the hallway when she opened the door.

"Miss Trent?" He sneaked a look at the list in his hand. "Everything okay? You like tea? Coffee?"

"No, thank you. I'm going out on deck and get some air."

He seemed to think that was very funny. "Lots of air out there," he said, gesturing toward the large porthole over one of the twin beds. "Maybe more than you want."

"That's what I'm afraid of," she acknowledged. "At least it can't get rough until we reach the open sea."

He consulted his watch. "Twenty minutes, maybe thirty. After we drop the pilot. How about early coffee?" Seeing her puzzled expression, he explained, "You like it served here before breakfast? All you do is tell me."

"No, thanks."

"Tea?"

"I don't think so."

"We'll see."

Abby wasn't sure how he meant that and his smooth face didn't give anything away. He put a big check on his list, before turning to leave. "I come back later in case you change your mind."

"That isn't necessary," she assured him. "You won't have to bother."

"No trouble." He paused as a deep-throated signal came from one of the tugs alongside.

Abby's attention was on their departure and she started over to try and see what was happening through the porthole. "Whatever you think," she agreed carelessly, and registered his satisfied murmur and the closing of the stateroom door without looking round.

The big hotels on the slight hills ringing Hamilton harbor were already starting to slide past as the tugs turned the *Southern Cross*, getting her out of the berth and then nudging her toward the channel.

It was frustrating to have such a limited view of the goings-on, Abby decided, and checked to make sure that she'd put her stateroom key in her jacket before going out and closing the door.

The narrow Sun Deck corridor was completely deserted, but the sound of voices and piped-in cabin music filtered from behind stateroom doors as she moved toward the stern of the ship. Surely there couldn't be many people there, she thought. Not away from the main lounge or the veranda grill two decks down, where a buffet was being served for all passengers who'd missed lunch ashore.

Abby pushed her way through a heavy metal door at the end of the corridor and was met with a shower of rain as she stepped out onto the open deck. She winced and turned up the collar of her jacket, looking for shelter.

There was some sort of a storage locker on the narrow walkway toward the bow. It was built with an overhang—just big enough for Abigail to huddle under. Fortunately, there wasn't a soul in that part of the deck and she had an uninterrupted view of the small islands in the Great Sound. Peering out toward the stern gained her another faceful of rain, but she could see the hotels and houses on the hillsides of Paget and Warwick, where an occasional dark green patch identified a golf course. She stepped back under her metal cover out of the rain again and thought how fortunate that she was on the wrong side of the ship to see Blair's waterfront apartment-hotel or the luxurious complex where she'd been registered. It was easier to stare at the small islets they were passing to the west, which were blessedly anonymous. A few boasted magnificent homes and private docks so that their owners could get easily across to Hamilton, but most were simply blobs of green vegetation with navigational warning signals posted on their rocky outreaches. Looking through the overcast toward the fingers of land which housed the American Naval Air Station, she saw another cruise liner at anchor in Little Sound. There was smoke coming from the funnel, though, so it probably would be sailing shortly, as well.

Like rats leaving, Abby thought unhappily, and then wished she'd avoided the comparison. There was no point in dwelling on sinking ships!

She huddled even deeper in her shelter as the rain poured down at a new angle when the *Southern Cross* changed course in the channel. There was still a fairly decent view of Ireland Island across the water to the north and west. The ragged silhouette of the Maritime Museum and the Keepyard at the very end of land triggered another memory. What would happen to the perfume factory now? Its new owner was going to have a different business address—if those last moments at St. George were any indication of things to come. The samples of fragrance she'd been given might be the last shipment for some time. At that point, she simply didn't care. All of her rational thinking must have stopped hours before.

She shook her head impatiently when she realized she was moping again. Fairly floundering in self-pity. And if she were going to do that, she might as well have stayed in the stateroom instead of freezing on an open deck.

She started back toward the door leading into the corridor. When she reached the stern, the open deck allowed her to see across to the other side of the ship. At that moment, the *Southern Cross* shifted to a northeast course to avoid the coral reef which had caused disaster to so many early navigators. That meant one more view of St. George's, Abby thought, staying glued to her place. Would Blair still be out there—perhaps watching the liner come up the last part of the channel before turning out into open ocean?

The possibility was enough to keep her standing there for the next half-hour as the green coastline slipped smoothly by. The white-roofed houses, the enchanting coves and beaches, even the steady stream of airplanes leaving the island from Kindley Field held her spellbound.

The ship veered away from land just before the buildings and hotels of St. George's Island appeared. A few minutes later, the engines of the *Southern Cross* slowed and the swells of the Atlantic could be felt as the big liner wallowed in the troughs.

They must be taking off the pilot, Abby thought, coming out of her transfixed state when the lessened vibration finally sank into her consciousness. Thrusting her hands in her jacket pockets, she went out into the rainy drizzle to look over the rail. Sure enough, a black-hulled boat with the white letters "PILOT" on the side was even then nudging the liner up toward the bow. There was a figure wearing oilskins on deck, gesturing to the man in the wheelhouse, while, far above them on the bridge of the *Southern Cross*, Abby could see two ship's officers watching the maneuvering. On the promenade deck below, there were still a few hardy passengers following the exchange as well, willing to risk the dampness for drama as the pilot left the liner to go down the dangling rope ladder onto the deck of the smaller boat.

It was always fascinating to watch, but at that moment a dark cloud overhead took its revenge and dumped a cascade of rain over the ships. Abigail's jacket and scarf were no match for it and she scurried toward a covered stair and the deck below.

Halfway down, she tried to brush the moisture from her jacket and pulled the sodden scarf from her head. The smell of food wafted up the stairs and, when she reached the lower deck, she discovered a barbecue being served under a canopy at the edge of the swimming pool.

Even the appetizing-looking hamburgers weren't enough to counteract the dampness seeping into her jacket and Abby went through double doors to another lounge, where even more passengers were at a long buffet.

By then, Abby decided that a cup of coffee might be therapeutic as well as helping to pass the time. Besides, she told herself wryly, there was no use hurrying back to that empty stateroom upstairs just to do some unpacking.

A cursory glance through the wide windows at the side of the lounge showed the gray Atlantic swells slipping steadily by again. The increased engine vibration under her feet would have confirmed it—even without checking the scenery. Almost against her will, she looked toward the windows on the other side of the lounge then and discovered that the last bit of Bermuda had disappeared; the *Southern Cross* was well and truly on her journey.

Abigail served herself from a gleaming urn of coffee and took her steaming cup to an empty table, getting as far as possible away from the chattering, lighthearted groups of her fellow passengers. A ship's news bulletin was being distributed to everyone, announcing the activities which the *Southern Cross*'s social staff had hurriedly assembled to cope with the early sailing.

Abby read through the afternoon's list of bingo, backgammon lessons, and an extra complimentary ballroom-dance session with loathing—wondering why she'd let herself be talked into a solitary shipboard passage. As the big liner changed course again and sent her coffee splashing into the saucer, her lips suddenly clamped into a tight line. If she didn't get back to the stateroom and swallow some motion-sickness pills, she'd never stay vertical long enough to complain about dinner—by the time it came along!

She'd shoved back her chair and prudently put her coffee cup in the middle of the table so that it wouldn't slide off when she noticed her bedroom steward coming toward her, a relieved grin on his face.

"I'm glad to find you, Miss Trent. When I was in your stateroom just now, a message arrived."

She stood up, immediately visualizing all sorts of disasters. "Oh, Lord! Thanks for letting me know. Did you bring it with you?"

"I wasn't sure I'd find you." He spread his hands in an apologetic gesture. "It seemed safer to leave it in the stateroom."

"Yes, of course." She summoned a smile and reached for her purse. "I'll go back and see what it is."

All her other worries disappeared completely as she hurried toward the main companionway to get back up a deck to her stateroom. The liner's up-and-down movement forced her to hang on to the stair railing and finally slow her pace as she started down the long narrow corridor.

When she turned into the short hallway, her eyes widened as she saw her door sway with the motion of the ship. Evidently the steward had been in such a hurry to find her that he'd neglected to lock up when he'd left.

She was halfway over the threshold, her worried gaze sweeping the bureau for the radiogram, before she noticed that while she'd been on deck, the steward had pulled the curtains partway over the portholes. Together with the rainy weather outside, it left the stateroom almost dark. She reached for the light switch on the doorjamb but suddenly her fingers stilled as she saw a tall figure loom up from the chair beyond the bureau.

"Dear God, what's happening?" Her words were a thready whisper as she swayed, clutching the metal door edge.

Blair caught her when she would have fallen. "Good Lord! You can't faint now!" he said in a ragged deep voice. He nudged the light switch with his elbow and looked around for a place to put her.

His astringent tone was more effective than anything else to put the stiffening back in Abby's body. She struggled from his clasp and faced him angrily—all the frustrations that had plagued her since they'd parted suddenly spilling out.

"You have a hell of a nerve sneaking in here—scaring the life out of me! Why couldn't you have told me you were aboard like any sensible person?" She plunged on, knowing if she succumbed to the light-headed relief that his appearance had triggered, she'd be clinging to his neck and making an utter fool of herself again. "That would be the decent thing to do, instead of sitting around in the dark—waiting to pounce. Just . . . just"— she gestured helplessly as she tried to find words— "just making yourself at home."

"But why shouldn't I?"

His drawled assertion sliced into her anger like a steel blade. As she stood staring up at him, eyes wide in her pale face, he went on calmly, "I have a perfect right to be here. After all, it *is* my stateroom."

Chapter Ten

"*Your* stateroom?"

The obvious distress in Abby's voice and the way she gripped the closet door for support would have thawed any man's resistance.

Blair was quick to abandon continued hostilities. "Maybe we could sit down and talk this over like two civilized people," he said coaxingly. When she nodded and sank onto the edge of the nearest bed, he started to sit beside her. Then, instead, he carefully went over to the upholstered chair across the room.

Abigail bit the edge of her lip. His deliberate move was an echo of the past and probably an omen of things to come. Which wasn't surprising, she told herself fiercely, considering the welcome she'd given him. She spoke up before she lost her nerve. "I'm sorry I was such a horror just now. It was so dim in here that I thought I was seeing things. Then, when it really turned out to be you, I wondered if I'd gone round the bend. There was no way you could get aboard in Hamilton unless"—she looked at him hopefully—"unless you came on the ship before I did."

He grinned and shook his head.

"No?" She managed a tremulous smile in response. "Maybe I should pinch you to find out if I *am* dreaming."

"The hell with that! We have better things to do." He sighed then and rested his head against the stateroom wall, looking like a man who'd had a hard day but was well content with his new surroundings.

"You didn't walk on water?" Abby went on determinedly, strangely reluctant to dwell on those "better things." Seeing the sudden gleam in his eyes, she shook her head. "Scratch that one. I refuse to play twenty questions any longer. How in the dickens did you manage it?"

"The pilot boat, of course. I wondered if you were one of those onlookers lining the rail—hoping I'd fall off the rope ladder in the transfer."

"Surely not hoping," she said, pretending to be shocked. Her lips curved as she thought about it. "Did you?"

"Did I what?"

"Drop off the ladder."

"Certainly not. What bloodthirsty creatures you women are."

"I thought this was going to be a friendly discussion."

"You're right." He put up both hands in surrender. "I promise to stay away from controversy."

"At least for the next five minutes or until I object to

your ordering me around." She kept her tone severe. "You can't be serious about this stateroom."

"Why not? This was the only vacant cabin—in fact, they've assigned two perfectly healthy passengers to the hospital just so they'd have a place to sleep. And don't get any bright ideas—there aren't any extra beds down there now. We'd both have been out of luck if the purser weren't a friend of mine."

"I see." Abigail kept her expression noncommittal although her thoughts were racing madly. Since they'd managed to share the same roof in Bermuda, she'd be foolish to act Victorian about a few more nights. "Well, we're both adults," she began, only to have him cut in.

"The phrase is 'two consenting adults.' Not that it matters," he added, shrugging.

"I should think it would matter a great deal."

"You're getting mad again," he reminded her.

She opened her mouth and then closed it, counting five slowly before she said, "If you want to improve my disposition, you could start by answering some questions."

He shifted his hips in the chair and stretched long legs out on the stateroom carpet. "All right, shoot. What do you want to know?"

"Everything, of course," she said, wishing she *could* pinch him. He was deliberately stalling, she was sure of it. "Start at the beginning. What happened in St. George after I left?"

"Your friend Ian was taken into custody. But that's hardly the beginning."

"And you can hardly call him my friend," she said

primly. "He rates right along with Maida and St. John. Of course, I'm sure that Maida had redeeming qualities."

"Lots of them," Blair concurred, keeping his tone solemn. Then he grinned slowly. "The authorities had decided early on that Mrs. Collins had too lavish a bankroll, considering her way of life. I was assigned to try and get some answers."

"Hardship duty if I ever heard of it," Abby said dryly. "How did she get in the bird-refuge business?"

"Well"—Blair seemed to be searching for the right words—"I needed an assistant . . ."

"Don't say any more. I have an excellent imagination."

"I swear that I kept my fingers crossed every time she came near."

It was hard for Abby to hide her elation at that news. She wrapped her arms over her breasts as a shiver coursed through her body, and then realized it wasn't happiness causing the reaction; she was darned near freezing.

Blair got to his feet, frowning, as he diagnosed the trouble. "Is that jacket as damp as your hair?"

"It's just started to soak through." She stood up beside him to peel it off. "Could you turn up the heat? Or is there a thermostat?"

"Of course there is," he said, finding the dial nearby and hearing a satisfying noise as he rotated it. "Usually they're painted on, but this one really works. I imagine the steward turned down the heat when they were in port. Once you get out of those wet clothes, you'll feel better."

She reached for her suitcase and put it on top of the nearest bed. "At least this time I can't blame it on the humidity."

"What have you been doing since you got aboard? You must have been standing out on an open deck to get that wet."

Abby had no intention of confessing that she'd been doing just that—mainly because she'd been missing him so badly that the thought of sitting alone in the stateroom was intolerable. "It *is* raining," she said, "and I needed some fresh air. What do I change into?" The last came as she extracted some dresses from her case and put them on hangers in the closet.

He shrugged and sat back down in his chair, pulling off his tie and tossing it in the direction of his suitcase. "Do you have a special outfit for unpacking? I suppose that's next on the agenda." He leaned back, obviously not planning to do *his* unpacking anytime in the near future. "Put on that robe of yours—it might not be sexy, but it should keep you warm."

She pulled out the terry-cloth robe and surveyed it. "It's not that bad."

"It's not bad at all. That's the trouble. Look, are you going to just stare at it or put it on?"

Abby gave him an exasperated look, knowing how he'd react if she asked him to close his eyes. There was nothing for it but to change in that tiny bathroom. They'd certainly have to work out a schedule for any continued coexistence. "I'm going," she said, snatching up the robe, as he made a threatening move. "I'll leave the door ajar so you can go on with your story. What happened to Brian St. John?"

"He's in custody with his boss. We had him salted away earlier at the gallery—waiting for Ian to show up.

Woodbourne must have gotten wind of it. When you appeared on the scene, he decided a hostage would help get him off the island. What the devil were you doing there in the first place?"

"I wanted to buy my Burns print before I sailed." At his exasperated sigh, she stuck her flushed face around the bathroom door. "Why couldn't you tell me that you suspected them? Didn't you trust me?"

"Of course I did." He stood up and walked over to the door which she'd left ajar. "Hand out your wet clothes. I'll put them on a hanger in the closet to dry. And use a towel on your hair. If you get pneumonia out of this lot . . ."

". . . I'll be in a bad way." Her voice mocked him. "Especially with no beds left in the hospital. Here's my laundry." Her jacket and skirt came around the doorjamb.

"What about your blouse?"

Her arm emerged again—this time with a blouse. "You make me feel like a striptease dancer—handing things out around a curtain," Abby said as she appeared suddenly in the thigh-length terry robe.

Blair's glance was assessing, before he turned to the closet and started hanging up her clothes. "You sure as hell don't look like one."

"Good!" Abby tried to sound as if she meant it, leaving the bathroom door wide open as she toweled her hair. "Why didn't you warn me about Ian and St. John last night?"

"Because I didn't tumble to Ian's connection with any of this until you mentioned seeing him with the other two at that perfume factory."

"You mean at our Chinese dinner?"

"That's right. Something good had to come out of it,"
Blair said ruefully. "The air-cargo job was a perfect
cover for his frequent comings and goings. But until
you sighted him at the perfume place, Woodbourne had
been careful to stay clear of St. John and Maida. When
you mentioned a new owner and that he was chauffeuring them about at the other end of the island, it put a
new slant on things. And that, together with his sudden
interest in you, sent us back to our homework."

Blair sat down in the chair again and faced her
squarely. "Even so, it took us most of the night to piece
the evidence together so we could make the charges
stand. There's no doubt that he's the head of the
operation, and this time Woodbourne will need a very
astute defense lawyer."

"I'm glad," she said simply. "The way he acted at the
garden this morning showed how ruthless he could be.
I'll bet they'll dig up all sorts of unsavory bits in his
background." She gave her hair a last rub and turned to
hang the towel on a hook, reaching for her comb
afterward.

"Well, if he doesn't cooperate, I imagine that St. John
and Maida will," Blair concurred. "They were in it for
the money and now that there isn't any future payoff,
they'll be anxious to shift all the blame possible on
Woodbourne to save their own necks."

Abby decided her hair didn't look too bad and she
put the comb on a shelf in the medicine cabinet. After
tightening the belt on her robe, she went back in the
stateroom and sank onto the edge of the nearest bed.

"Feel better?" Blair wanted to know.

"Yes, thanks." For no logical reason, she felt suddenly shy under his level gaze, and she fumbled again with the belt at her waist.

"Warm enough?"

She nodded and thought about shoving the pillows up against the headboard so that she could lean back and be comfortable, but there was something about Blair's surveillance that made her decide against it. Her cheeks took on added color as she saw his slow smile. Damn the man! He was back to mind reading again!

She took a deep breath and tried to sound businesslike. "I'd like to send a thank-you note to Zeke. His turning up at the church when he did this morning certainly saved my bacon. I don't suppose that was a coincidence either."

"Well, Zeke wasn't. We just didn't expect to find you there."

She ignored his last remark. "Then he isn't a taxi driver? Not that there's anything wrong with driving a taxi, but . . . I wish you'd stop looking so amused at everything I say!"

"It's just that you rise to the bait so beautifully." He waved a placating hand when she reached for a pillow to throw. "Okay, I'll stop. Besides, you were right about Zeke. It's Detective Sergeant Ezekiel Smith, actually. He was keeping an eye on you while you were on the island. Why do you suppose his taxi was available way out at Somerset when you decided to leave that bus?"

"I should have known," she said slowly.

Blair shook his head. "No, not really. If you lived in

Bermuda, you would have. But as a casual visitor, it was safe enough. And he thoroughly enjoyed the duty—even to looking for your orange cat in the rain."

"He must have thought I was crazy."

"Well, if he did, he didn't show it. As a matter of fact, he sent a message to you. Apparently he went back to the hotel grounds the first thing this morning and found the cat. When he made inquiries and discovered it didn't belong to anybody, he took it home—so that story has a happy ending."

"How marvelous!"

"Unfortunately, I can't promise anything as good on your Burns print," Blair told her ruefully. "It was hardly the time to be buying pictures when we had the place staked out this morning. However, if we go back as trial witnesses, there's no reason we can't check the market for a print then. From a reputable dealer this time." Her stunned expression made him ask, "What's the matter now?"

"You said 'we' might have to go back as witnesses. Are you serious?"

"There's a good possibility. Why? It should be a relatively painless procedure."

"You don't understand," she pressed on. "In my job, I can't just up and leave."

He pretended to consider as he watched her, his eyes lazy, teasing slits. "Then maybe it would be better all around if you found another job."

The calm assumption that he could order her life around just as it suited his convenience brought her pride to the fore. "You make it sound so easy. Ever since I arrived, you've been telling me what to do—like your favorite robot."

"And you've been fighting back every inch of the way," he said dryly.

She got up from the bed, stung by his injustice. "What did you expect?"

"Maybe a little cooperation. Or is that too much to hope for?"

"You're damned right it is! Now that all the fuss is over, you've finally found a day or two to fit me into your life. That's why you've arranged this cozy little stateroom for two. And I'm supposed to be grateful for"—she gulped as tears threatened—"for whatever you can offer. Talk about high-handed male despots! You'd win the prize hands down!"

He surged to his feet then and caught her when she would have turned away, forcing her to look up at him. "You little idiot! Is that what you think?"

"Let go, damn you!" She struggled futilely, trying to escape from his iron grip, and then sagged against him, resting her head on his chest. "Oh, why don't you let me alone? I can't take much more of this."

Her struggles to get loose had pulled her robe from one shoulder, showing an expanse of satinlike skin. Almost as if he couldn't help it, Blair slowly lowered his head and rested his lips against it.

Abby moaned as she felt his touch, and pressed her face against his shirtfront. For an instant she was tempted to unbutton it, letting her own lips feel the warmth of his tanned skin. Then belatedly she came to her senses and pushed back from his clasp. "Please don't, Blair," she said, trying to stop his hands as they moved caressingly over her. "Next you'll be saying that this is all a mistake and you should have known better. Like the last time you kissed me. The first time, too—if it comes to that."

"And I was right." Blair looked down at her whimsically. He pulled the robe back into place, as if honor-bound to bundle her up like a puritan, even arranging the lapels to hide the glimpse of shadowed cleavage that had intrigued him. "If you want to keep this conversation on a higher plane, then you'll have to make a few running repairs. You can start by getting some clothes on," he said, ignoring her accusations.

"But *you're* the one who insisted I take them off."

"And it won't be the last time," he said obliquely. "For Lord's sake, sit down—no, not on that bed . . ." He put his hands at her waist and calmly deposited her in the chair he'd been occupying. "If we're going to talk about kissing, it's better to stay away from mattresses."

Abby shook her head, unable to hide her anguish any longer. "I'm not in the mood for one of your lectures, Blair. Not now. Not ever again."

He made a helpless gesture. "I wish you'd trust me. This isn't a lecture. Believe it or not, I'm trying to explain." When he saw her relax slightly in the chair, he went on—his voice deeper than she'd ever heard it. "The first time I kissed you at Jonas' house—it was strictly an impulse. I'd wanted to for weeks—ever since that day Jonas had introduced us and you stared down your beautiful little nose at me. Only there wasn't any future in getting to know you then, so it seemed best not to start anything."

"But the night you drove me home, you behaved like a . . . a . . ."

He seemed amused by her vehemence. "Beast?"

"Exactly. Stop laughing—I don't think it's funny. I didn't then, either," she added, remembering that night so long ago.

"Things got a little out of hand. When we arrived at the house, I thought I was entitled to a simple good-night kiss. How did I know what it was going to turn into?"

"Then I wasn't the only one?"

"To be left reeling?" He shook his head. "At least you had the excuse of too much champagne. I was cold sober, without a permanent job, and scheduled to leave town in the morning. Not only that, you told me that you couldn't stand the sight of me—or words to that effect."

"I was lying in my teeth," Abby said, unable to cling to her feminine pride any longer.

"And all I wanted to do was throw you over my shoulder and head for the nearest cave," he said, with a glance that sent a warmth of yearning through her. "Instead I had to depend on Jonas for news of you after that."

"I didn't know—he didn't say a word about it."

"I'd have had his head if he'd tried." Blair's tone was fierce suddenly, as he sat down on the bed.

"But what if I'd fallen in love with someone else?"

"Did you?"

She thrilled at his darkening glance, but didn't waste any time reassuring him. "Of course not. You very neatly spoiled any other man for me—even when you were thousands of miles away. I wonder if Jonas suspected it when I mentioned a Bermuda vacation?"

"Of course he did! That old fox! And he knew that I wanted to see you, so he insisted on your delivering that report. That way, we were sure to get together. What none of us knew," Blair added ruefully, "was that you'd be attacked and almost killed as soon as you arrived." He rubbed his fingers along his jaw. "It was a nightmare from the start."

"And I felt you couldn't wait to send me home again because of Maida."

"That's what I suspected. Look, love, put yourself in my place." Blair's hand raked through his hair. "And I wish to God you would!"

His distrait tone, so much at variance with his usual calm assurance, made Abby say warily, "Would what?"

"I'm sick of long-distance explanations." He patted the bed beside him. "Come over here. That's *much* better," he added, pulling her across his lap when she obediently came across and sat next to him. He bent to nuzzle the soft skin below her ear and let his lips trail down to the hollow of her throat. He started to investigate further and then groaned, raising his head. "Oh, hell! I suppose you want to hear the rest of the story."

"Maybe we'd better." Abby was so breathless by then that she could hardly get the words out.

"You're right. Otherwise it'll be a long time before we get around to it. What's left to tell?"

"Maida?" Abigail asked tremulously, and felt her last suspicion disappear when Blair grimaced and shook his head.

"Part of the job, that's all. I don't like sleek brunettes. My tastes run to coppery-gold witches who can't keep their pajamas buttoned properly. It's just a good thing that you had that lump on your head to help protect your maidenly charms."

"You were so noble that I wondered what I'd done wrong," Abby told him severely. "I'm glad you're reverting to type. What do we do now?"

Blair stared down at her flushed cheeks as if thoroughly enjoying the view. "I know what I'd like to do."

She struggled to escape, but not very hard, subsiding quite happily when he merely tightened his clasp. "*You're* the one who arranged to share this stateroom," she pointed out, "and it's a long way to New York."

"Ummm, I know." His mouth moved lightly over her brows, and down her silken cheek to stop at the corner of her lips, punctuating his words nicely. "I've had a devil of a time keeping my hands off you ever since you arrived in Bermuda. And if you think I can share this room and stay away from you three more days, you're crazy. That's why I arranged with my friend the purser to have one of the passengers meet us in the chapel in about fifteen minutes from now. Where are you going?"

Abby had scrambled to her knees. "What did you say?"

Blair's grin was wide and teasing. "Just that there's a nice old Anglican clergyman who's going to meet us with a special marriage license and say the magic words.

The captain's busy with his hurricane, and besides, this is much more legal." Blair sobered suddenly and got to his feet, pulling her up beside him. "I didn't take too much for granted, did I, dearest? You will marry me?"

Abigail had to swallow before she could answer, but the dawning joy in her face told him what he wanted to know, even before she said, "Oh, yes! I do love you so."

"Good!" He started to kiss her and then put her safely at arm's length. "There's plenty of time for that later. You'd better put some clothes on . . ."

She laughed and started to slip off her robe, heading for the closet. "You keep telling me that."

"You'll probably never hear it again during our long married life," Blair said fervently. "But we're keeping that appointment in the chapel in fifteen minutes—even if I have to carry you wrapped in a sheet."

Abby lingered in the bathroom doorway to give him a cheeky grin. "Promises . . . promises. That's what I get."

Blair moved quickly before she could escape, and drew her close, letting her feel his strength. "Just one promise, darling. All my love for the rest of my life. Will that do?"

His touch made her shiver with delight and she stood on tiptoe to kiss him. "Dearest Blair," she whispered softly, "it won't be nearly long enough."

About the Author

Glenna Finley is a native of Washington State. She earned her degree from Stanford University in Russian Studies and in Speech and Dramatic Arts, with emphasis on radio.

After a stint in radio and publicity work in Seattle, she went to New York City to work for NBC as a producer in its international division. In addition, she worked with the "March of Time" and *Life* magazine.

As a producer, she had her own show about activities in Manhattan, a show that was broadcast to England. The programs were similar to those of the "Voice of America."

Though her life in New York was exciting, she eventually returned to the Northwest where she married. Currently residing in Seattle with her husband, Donald Witte, and their son, she loves to travel, and draws heavily on her travels and experiences for the novels that have been published. Her books for NAL have sold several million copies.

SIGNET Books by Glenna Finley

(0451)

- [ ] **THE MARRIAGE MERGER** (117182—$1.95)*
- [ ] **WILDFIRE OF LOVE** (114914—$1.95)*
- [ ] **BRIDAL AFFAIR** (114965—$1.95)
- [ ] **THE CAPTURED HEART** (114906—$1.95)
- [ ] **KISS A STRANGER** (112288—$1.95)
- [ ] **LOVE FOR A ROGUE** (113152—$1.95)
- [ ] **LOVE IN DANGER** (091906—$1.75)
- [ ] **LOVE'S HIDDEN FIRE** (114981—$1.95)
- [ ] **LOVE LIES NORTH** (114922—$1.95)
- [ ] **LOVE'S MAGIC SPELL** (114892—$1.95)
- [ ] **A PROMISING AFFAIR** (079175—$1.50)
- [ ] **THE RELUCTANT MAIDEN** (098633—$1.75)
- [ ] **THE ROMANTIC SPIRIT** (114930—$1.95)
- [ ] **SURRENDER MY LOVE** (079167—$1.50)
- [ ] **TO CATCH A BRIDE** (115007—$1.95)
- [ ] **TREASURE OF THE HEART** (07324X—$1.25)
- [ ] **WHEN LOVE SPEAKS** (117999—$1.95)

*Price slightly higher in Canada

Buy them at your local bookstore or use this convenient coupon for ordering.

THE NEW AMERICAN LIBRARY, INC.,
P.O. Box 999, Bergenfield, New Jersey 07621

Please send me the books I have checked above. I am enclosing $_____
(please add $1.00 to this order to cover postage and handling). Send check
or money order—no cash or C.O.D.'s. Prices and numbers are subject to change
without notice.

Name_____

Address_____

City _____ State _____ Zip Code _____
Allow 4-6 weeks for delivery.
This offer is subject to withdrawal without notice.